Tales Of
MARITIME
MAINE

Tales Of
MARITIME
MAINE

The Vanished Years of the Maine Coast Brought to
Life in Three Absorbing Tales. By Bruce Clark

YANKEE BOOKS

A division of
Yankee Publishing Incorporated
Dublin, New Hampshire

Designed by Margo Letourneau
Yankee Publishing Incorporated
Dublin, New Hampshire

First Edition
Copyright 1987 by Bruce Clark

Library of Congress Catalogue Card Number: 86-51015

ISBN: 0-89909-122-9

CONTENTS

Part One

ANTHONY'S LUCK

hould it happen that you find yourself ashore on Winter Island, you may in conversation hear a reference to "Anthony's luck." Possibly by the context you will believe you understand; but it is very easy to be deceived. Anthony's luck is not really luck at all, you see, but a kind of faith in the future, a faith in a good beyond what is immediately apparent, a faith in something more than that which can be proven true.

Winter Islanders do not all profess to believe in Anthony's luck, but about everybody would like to believe in it. The phrase is part of the language on Winter Island, and is invoked by all regardless of professed opinion about the fate of Anthony Stilwell and Penny Dunning. The custom of picking some of "Penny's daisies," which grow on The Nubbin, a ledge in the harbor mouth, to bring this sort of luck to a marriage, a fishing trip, or a boat launching is universal.

It is easy to see why Winter Islanders would believe or want to believe in a higher or more permanent good than the world offers. Life on the island has never been easy and seldom safe. If there is any lesson this life instills it is wariness of the sea and of figuring too much on the future. To this day the uncertainties of the sea so control the actions of the islanders that anyone who lets on to know exactly what he is going to do in the next days or even hours is known dryly as being "pretty sure of himself."

What is not so easy to understand is why these people, who have so often been used hard by the sea, should have seen in the lives of Anthony Stilwell and Penny Dunning evidence of triumph rather than tragedy. Not easy to understand, that is, unless you have heard the story, which island children all know well by the age of five. . . .

Back in the 1860s and '70s, before the depression in the offshore fisheries of the '80s, which reduced Maine fishermen fishing Georges Bank to using sloops, and turned men in droves to lobstering, most fishermen used to go far out on the deep sea for their livelihood. From Winter Island, they went mostly in schooners, hand-lining from dories.

Wilbur Dunning was owner and captain of the *Almira Carswell Dunning*, a fast, tall-rigged, weatherly schooner of the Gloucester type. With a crew of island men, he would sail south to Georges Bank and stay until the *Almira*'s hold was full of salt fish, mostly cod. When all his salt had been wetted, as the saying went, he would put in and sell his catch at the port where he thought he could get the best price, and then sail home.

So it was that on a cold September afternoon in 1865, Wilbur Dunning dropped anchor in Round Harbor on Winter Island and went ashore, after a three-month absence on the grounds. The sky was heavily overcast, and though it was not long after midday it was dim enough that lamplight glowed in the windows of some of the houses.

The burly young black-bearded captain strode up the path towards his small, neat, white-clapboarded house of four gables. He met several people on the way there whom he greeted in a voice of booming cheer, but each of these people failed to meet his eye when returning the greeting, looking elsewhere, such as at the schooner in the harbor or the bare granite showing through the thin soil where the path traversed.

The captain thought this behavior a little strange, but he was anxious to get home to Almira, his wife, whom he had met in Boston and married just this June and brought here to the home he had built on the island where he'd grown up. Whatever was bothering his neighbors was apparently common knowledge and Almira should be able to tell him about it as easily as anyone else.

Almira opened the door as he set his weight to the front steps. Her brown eyes were wide and round, and her delicate white hands entangled themselves in the golden chain around her neck as she stepped back to let him across the threshold.

He looked at her, grinning broadly through his wreath of beard, and stepped inside, banging the door shut after him with a casual swat of a big hand.

Almira had a lamp going in a niche above her sewing table, where she had been at work when he arrived. He looked at her haloed against the soft light, slim and lacy and delicate, and he said, "Well, don't be afraid, woman, come greet your husband!" and held out his huge arms welcomingly.

She allowed herself to be held, but she turned her head aside when he tried to kiss her. He thought she was being coy, and he took her face in both hands and looked her straight in the eye and kissed her firmly on the lips.

He asked then for news, wondering in the back of his mind if she would tell him she was carrying a child. She told him hesitantly of a baby born, someone who had died, and sicknesses that had come on some. None of it explained the greetings he had gotten from his neighbors, but he had had a very good fishing trip and he had been thinking about coming home to his wife almost since leaving her, and this was about all he cared to concern himself with for now.

It wasn't until that night that he finally learned what had happened. They lay in bed with the fires banked and the wind moaning under the eaves and the coverlid pulled up over them. Almira had made the coverlid in his absence and he was congratulating himself on his choice of a wife when she said, her voice choked, "Wilbur, there is something I have to tell you." It was pitch dark in the room, so he couldn't see her face, but he tried anyway. "Wilbur, I hope you can forgive me. I have been . . . unfaithful."

Wilbur turned his head to stare at the ceiling, trying to take in what his wife was saying.

"Can you forgive me?" she said, her voice so low as to be nearly inaudible.

"Who?" he demanded, when he had collected his wits. He felt as though he'd been belted in the middle by the main boom.

She was silent.

"*Who?*" he roared, and rolled from the bed, found a candle and lit it, holding it close to her white face.

"T- Mr. Carroll." Her hands bunched the edge of the coverlid under her chin.

"Tom Carroll!"

He stood thinking about Carroll. Carroll was the storekeeper on the island. Carroll was the one who, when all the other boys were going out with their fathers to learn to fish, or shipping as cabin boys, or lobstering, or running a sloop up and down all day while an older man fished from a dory or harpooned swordfish from the bowsprit, hung around the store playing pranks, stealing things from the shelves. Whenever his disgusted father tried to take him out on his boat, Tom Carroll would disappear and not come out of hiding until his father had gone. Later on, Carroll spent most of his time sparking the girls. For some reason, he was very popular with them, and you could nearly always see him parading around with at least two. He had a slick tongue and a line of chatter that you couldn't ever get ahead of no matter how hard you might try. He could always do you one better and leave you in the dust feeling like you'd stuck your foot down your throat. He'd started out working in the store, and now he owned it. As far as Wilbur knew, Tom Carroll had never left the island, had never even been in a boat at all.

"Can you forgive me?" Almira's voice quavered upwards, breaking.

Wilbur simply couldn't speak to her. He blew out the candle and got into bed. He did not touch his wife. He lay on his back staring up into the dark. He did not doze off until nearly morning. Off and on through the night he could feel the bed shake to his wife's silent sobs, but he just could not say a word to her.

He never did bring himself to say anything to her again, other than to ask her to do things that he could not assume she would do without his telling her to. She wept often for months after that, but gradually the weeping tapered off and she went listlessly about her work, the pain so obvious in her eyes that people avoided meeting her gaze.

Wilbur went fishing again not long after, choosing to go market boating out of Gloucester all winter, racing fresh fish to market, riding out winter gales, and pushing his boat and his crew hard. In those days, the fashion was speed, and seaworthiness was sacrificed more and more to this fashion with every new boat being built. Not a year went by but there were schooners lost — Gloucester lost one hundred men and boys a year. The competition was stiff, the trade dangerous. Those who valued their lives tended to either take to the inshore fisheries or go in the bankers, which were usually more burdensome vessels and better able to stand up to the rough weather on the banks. The bankers salted their catch on board and came in only when out of salt.

Wilbur had three close scrapes, but he and his crew of adventurous young men came home safe and sound and much better off than they had been before leaving. They dropped anchor in Round Harbor on April 22, 1866, and again Wilbur headed for home. This time he did not walk with a long bouncing stride, but with a shorter firm one, his face tired and weathered-looking. He was only twenty-six years old, but already there were a few grey hairs appearing.

Almira did not open the door when he arrived, and as soon as he stepped over the threshold he heard a sharp squall from upstairs and his wife's voice softly hushing it. They had told him on the dock that he'd been a father for over three weeks — and told him with a straight face, too, though they knew as well as he did that the father could as easily be Tom Carroll.

He licked his lips and followed the sounds and found his wife had made one of the bedrooms into a nursery. She was bending over a crib, singing softly to a small well-wrapped bundle which was now quiet.

She must have heard him, but she did not acknowledge his presence by turning to look. Wilbur stood looking on, the gall rising up his throat. This was not his child — he could never believe it was. He could not help thinking how he would have felt coming home to find his wife singing to *his* child.

He couldn't stand the sight of it, and he turned away. As his heavily booted feet hit the stairs, the baby began squalling again.

Wilbur had planned to stay home a while, plant corn and beans and potatoes and some other things around in the valley where he'd bought a piece of land for that purpose, and have Otis Ballou haul the schooner and do some repairs. He also had thought he might amuse himself in his spare time by buying a small boat and going lobstering, and maybe doing a little swordfishing as well.

But the bitterness of his home seemed too much, and he decided to leave money and sail his schooner elsewhere for repairs, then go fishing again on the banks, perhaps more market boating. It was a hard-driving life, and it kept his mind and body dog-tired all the time — kept his attention off his wife and Tom Carroll.

He sailed with a small crew to Bath on the Kennebec and had his schooner hauled for repairs at the Stinson yard. Then time lay on him heavy and useless, and he sought refuge in grog shops, drinking rum.

Penny Kimberly Dunning, as Almira named her daughter (Wilbur would not even look at her, let alone help to name her), seemed to develop normally for the first year or so, but then her mother began to worry that she was not learning to talk. Penny was five before she spoke her first word. After that it became evident that she knew as much how to talk as any reasonably intelligent child did at her age: she just chose not to most of the time.

She was sent to the island school, and she got good grades, but she never mixed well with the other children, and she never smiled. She remained silent unless it was necessary for her to speak.

She was a slightly built girl, like her mother in that respect, with a long serious face, and somewhat incongruously heavy eyebrows, much like Tom Carroll's. This resemblance to Tom gave rise to a good deal of private discussion, and in many minds settled the question of the girl's parentage.

People made an effort to be polite and helpful to Almira Dunning, and she was always invited to quilting bees, welcome at the Ladies' Sewing Circle, and included in the rounds of visiting. But she was not thought of warmly, and she knew it. She gradually withdrew from the society of the other women on the island and became as silent as her daughter, and her husband when he was home.

As the years went by and Penny grew up, Almira wasted away, going from slight and delicate to thin and weak. Penny took on more and more of the household work — doing it without complaint, enthusiasm, or comment — and Almira spent more and more time in bed or sitting in her rocking chair. Her skin became so transparent that blue veins showed through most everywhere. Her voice, on the rare occasions when she spoke, was hesitant and wavery.

The year Penny Dunning was nineteen, codfishing was in a bad slump and getting worse. This meant hard times for Winter Island, and, as elsewhere, sloops were replacing schooners. Wilbur's schooner was over twenty years old and showing her age. Her outdated design made her too slow to have any chance at top prices in the market boating business any longer, yet her hold was not big enough for her to successfully operate as a regular banker. She had been doing so poorly the last five years that Wilbur had trouble getting crews.

In that spring of 1885, Wilbur Dunning did not have the money to fit out his schooner for a trip to the banks. He bitterly blamed the expense of the endless succession of patent medicines Almira tried in an attempt to find a cure for her weakness and wasting, but others thought it a wonder his pocket had held out for so long, considering how much rum he drank. It had indeed been nearly ten years since Wilbur had gotten through a day without his rum.

Wilbur took his schooner to the mainland, and after some trouble found a buyer who wanted a boat for the kiln-wooding trade. He offered only half of what Wilbur believed the boat worth, but Wilbur was getting thirsty and wanted to close the deal so he could get to the nearest grog shop. The proceeds of the sale were little more than sufficient to pay his debts and buy a 38-foot Friendship sloop, in which he and his schooner crew sailed home.

It's a long way to Georges Bank from Winter Island in a small boat, so Wilbur, with a helper by the name of Gardner Hawkins, went just east of the island to some grounds closer by, though these were not as rich as Georges Bank. They would go out and catch what fish they could, salting them down, and then sell their catch to a flake yard on the mainland, spend a night there, and return to the island the following day. They did this all summer, catching hake for the fresh market in midsummer when the cod gave out. Wilbur never stayed ashore on the island any longer than he had to: no sooner had he landed than he was anxious to get going again.

Then November arrived. A series of gales struck, and Wilbur had to stay in port. There were four storms in a row, almost without letup, the last being an out-and-out northeaster. On the third day of this final storm Wilbur sat in his chair at the front window, as he had throughout this time of storms, looking out beyond the harbor of boats pitching in the heavy confused grey chop to the open sea where the wind carried streamers of spume from the tops of the waves. Wilbur sat with his fists on the arms of the rocker, in one fist a bottle of rum. The wind howled at the eaves and in the chimney, and the roar of the rote on the shores of the island seemed to be not just in the air but in the ground and in the very floor of the house.

Penny was silently cleaning on the other side of the room, moving briskly, efficiently. She ran the household now, for the most part.

The stairs creaked, just audible above the buffeting of the wind and spattering of rain against the windows. Neither Wilbur nor Penny paid any mind.

Almira came slowly down and began rummaging in the closet. She put on one of Wilbur's heavy woolen sea coats and then a pair of his heavy sea boots, both coat and boots much too large for her.

Penny watched her without change of expression, saying nothing.

Wilbur did not even turn to look at her.

She shuffled wearily to the front door, looked back once — saw Wilbur still gazing out the window, and Penny with her mouth firmly closed — and she made a small inarticulate sound deep in her throat and went out letting the wind slam the door shut with a violence that shook the whole building.

For a while she merely stood braced against the onslaught, and then she slowly moved off along the path.

Round Harbor on Winter Island is a bowl of rock, perhaps a quarter mile across, its eastern rim somewhat lower than the western, cleft so that it lets in the sea. The western side of the bowl rises into cliffs a hundred fifty feet high, but there is an area of several hundred acres shaped like a quarter moon between the cliffs and the harbor in which all of the people lived at that time. The majority of the houses were clustered in the village, and Wilbur Dunning's was one of these, at the northern end of town.

On the southern side of the harbor mouth is a bold headland faced with a huge block of weathered granite which drops straight into the sea. Low tide leaves it looking the same as at high tide, except for a skirt of rockweed and an incrustation of barnacles. It stands eighty feet above high water. The fore edge of the flat top of the block of granite is bare. Back from the edge there are wizened spruces twisted by the wind into bizarre shapes, the weather edge of the woods.

Almira Dunning took the path leading onto Southern Head. Many in town saw her go and wondered where she was headed in such weather and without oilskins. She had hardly been outside at all for years. Before she got far, her coat was soaked through and was so heavy on her that she staggered under the weight of it.

The path to Southern Head was used mostly by lovers and by those going to hunt goosetongue, crabs, raspberries, and blackberries. There was no one but Almira on it now. She emerged from the spruces on the top of the granite headland in full view of anyone in the village who cared to watch, staggering uncertainly against the wind and the blinding sheets of spray. The weather was thick, but since Southern Head was less than a quarter mile from the village,

Almira was plainly visible. From his window, Wilbur watched her through a haze of rum.

Below, the water was completely obscured by spume and spray. Heavy masses of spray rose periodically and blew over the top of the headland in plumes.

Almira stumbled, head down, to the edge of the drop and with a final effort jumped off.

Wilbur's bottle of rum fell and drained on the floor. Penny turned to look at him. His chin had lifted and his hands gripped the scrolls on the ends of the arms of his chair. She watched him from the dimness of the far corner of the room like a cat, and after he got up wild-eyed and grabbed oilskins and boots from the closet and hurried out, she watched him from the window through which he had been watching the harbor — and a pale and ghostly apparition she was there, too, said those who saw her. Neighbor women, who had seen Almira jump, and whose husbands were setting out to help Wilbur, came to comfort Penny; but she would not answer the door. She disappeared from the window when Wilbur disappeared into the woods on the Southern Head path.

By the time the men returned hours later with her mother's broken and battered body, talking of how lucky they were to retrieve the body at all, Penny had cleaned up the spilled rum, tidied up her mother's room, stored away her mother's clothes, and prepared a place in the parlor for the body to be laid. Some thought her cold, a few thought the devil was in her, but most pitied her so much they hardly spoke of it.

Before his wife's suicide, Wilbur Dunning never spoke of his family troubles, though he was occasionally heard to curse the burden and expense of his wife's invalidism. He might have remained close-mouthed on the subject after Almira's death but for something Penny did.

One day in December, when he was back from a fishing trip and it was snowing, the flakes drifting down through the nearly still air with the peculiar silence only a windless snowfall can have, Wilbur was sitting at his window drinking rum. It was the middle of the afternoon and he had been drinking heavily all day in his brooding silent way, his eyes getting glassier and his hands shaking just a little.

Penny had been working in the kitchen, but now she took up her knitting and pulled the straight-backed wicker chair up from the chimney corner and sat beside Wilbur. This was something she had never done before. Wilbur took a pull on his rum. Penny sat straight of back, her hands moving quickly and rhythmically.

For some time they sat this way, neither looking at the other. Wilbur drank rum and Penny's needles clicked. Outside, the snow came down with such steadiness that it almost seemed the earth rose to meet it.

Wilbur flung his rum bottle, still a quarter full, across the room so it smashed against the white wainscotting.

Penny's needles stopping clicking and she looked up, mouth opening a little. Then she knitted another few strokes, and then she abruptly got up, putting her knitting in her chair, and cleaned up the mess.

Wilbur glared at her through bleary eyes. When she had finished the cleanup, she returned to her chair and once again began to knit.

Wilbur gripped the arms of his chair, glaring out at the veil of snow. After a while, Wilbur got up and pulled on a coat and went out and down to the landing. He climbed into his peapod and rowed out over the smooth glassy backs of the long low swells coming into the harbor from the sea. He tied the peapod to a shroud of his sloop and went aboard. He spent the rest of the day there, puttering.

Two days after this, Wilbur's helper on the boat, Gardner Hawkins, came to see when Wilbur thought he might head to the fishing grounds again. Gardner was a jolly, loud-voiced man of about forty; big, strong, slope-shouldered, well known to be somewhat henpecked. The door was opened to him by Penny.

"Well, how are ye, Penny?" he said with his broad, beaming smile, curling the brim of his old felt hat in his big hands, peering down at her.

She did not answer, smile, or change expression — she never did, though Gardner always greeted her cheerily. She just stepped back to let him in and then shut the door after him.

Wilbur was sitting in his chair by the window, putting hooks on a tub full of line. Beside him on the floor was the ever-present bottle of rum. He looked up with a challenging glare at Gardner. Penny removed some sewing from a wicker chair next to Wilbur's and left the room. Gardner sat down, leaning forward with his elbows on his knees to look at the line in the tub.

"Right smart of line there," he said.

Wilbur said nothing.

"Well, I guess the snow's over for now," Gardner said.

Wilbur grunted.

Gardner rubbed his jaw, wondering whether he ought to go. Wilbur was in one of his moods.

"Well," Gardner said, standing up, "I just thought I'd come see when you had in mind to go out again for some more haddies."

"Dunno," Wilbur said. "Soon."

"Well then," Gardner said. "You let me know. I'll be going now."

Gardner got as far as the door before Wilbur spoke.

"Penny ain't my daughter," Wilbur said bluntly.

Gardner didn't know quite what to say. It was accepted as fact by nearly everybody that Wilbur believed Penny was not his daughter, but the thing had never before been heard from his own mouth that Gardner knew of. Gardner looked at the door and tried to think what he ought to say.

"She's Tom Carroll's," Wilbur said. "It's well nigh time he took responsibility for her. I don't see no reason why *I* ought to have to see to her. She ain't none of *mine*. I been feedin' her and clothin' her these many years, but she *ain't* no kin of mine. I tell you, I don't want her in my house. I want her *out*. That Tom Carroll had ought to take hold of his responsibilities and provide for her."

Gardner Hawkins was never sure afterwards just what if anything he said to Wilbur that day, but when he left Wilbur's house he felt a heavy burden. One reason was that as he left he happened to catch a glimpse of Penny sitting quietly in the next room, surely having heard, and it made him wonder what talk like this must do to her. The other reason was the custom among the islanders relating to situations where one man had a grievance against another. The man with the grievance would tell a third party the complaint, and then this third man would tell the man against whom the complaint was lodged, usually over a period of time, little by little, in conversations about other things. Then a response would come back to the aggrieved man by the same route. Gardner Hawkins knew it was up to him to tell Tom Carroll that Wilbur wanted him to take Penny off his hands.

Gardner didn't say anything to Tom about it for almost three weeks. Then, returned from a fishing trip with Wilbur, he went to the store to be measured for some new boots by the cobbler who came around once a year to Winter Island; and afterwards he went out back to help Tom move some crates of dried goods around and got to talking to him about how the fishing was getting so bad he was thinking about going lobstering instead, and he mentioned how Wilbur didn't seem to be shaking off his mood much these days; and he said that he thought it had to do with Penny.

He hinted this way and that for about two months, and finally Tom said to him one day, "Just what is it you're suggesting, Gardner?"

They were sitting alone in the store with their feet up to the stove while a February blizzard went on outside. Tom was a skinny little man with a nervous way about him. His eyes never would rest steadily on anybody or anything. He had a temper, Gardner well knew, which was one thing that had made this hard. It always seemed one of the great mysteries to Gardner that this was a man who held great appeal for the women on the island, even now. Even more puzzling was that a man who liked the ladies so much and was so well-liked by them had never married.

"Well, Tom," Gardner said at length, drawing on his pipe, "it appears that Wilbur has got it in his head that you are Penny's father, and he won't let go of it."

Tom's feet came down firmly on the floor, and he got up.

"I know he always thought that, and everybody else thinks so too. But there's no truth in it at all." He clanked open the stove door, peered in and tossed in another chunk of dried oak and shut the door again. "You tell him that. You tell him I don't know if he's her father or not, but I know I'm not."

"Well," Gardner said, staring in embarrassment at his feet on the worn rail of the stove, "he don't say much about it, but he is worked up about it, you can tell. He thinks you're Penny's father, and he said you ought to take her in and support her." Gardner hunched his shoulders up and down quickly and shifted in his chair as though he'd eased into some position that twinged a nerve. He didn't look at Tom.

Tom walked to the counter and back again, limber-legged.

"That fellow's daft," Tom said tightly. "You know what it is? It's that that girl never says anything to anybody, never mixes with young folks; and she's cold as she can be to any young fellow who shows any interest in her. I never seen her smile, and I never heard tell of anybody else seeing it either. And if that weren't enough she's got to go capering around in the woods on all fours like an animal. Well, you know how it is with her. She won't be likely to get married off.

"Wilbur can see all this just as easy as you or I can, and it makes him all bothered that Penny will be in his house as long as he lives; but if he had any sense, he would take it as a thing for the best for him. It may be Penny's not just right in the head, but she's not dangerous; and they say she keeps that house up clean's a whistle inside and she can cook. Wilbur needs somebody looking after him. But some folks can't see good fortune if they trip over it."

"Well," Gardner said, "I don't know why he wants her out of his house, but he does. Maybe he wants to marry again. Not that I know about any woman he might be sparking."

"Why it'd be downright improper for me to take her in. Unless I married her. I'd have to marry her. Think how folks would talk if I weren't married to her."

Gardner decided not to point out that Tom had himself only just a couple of minutes ago complained that everybody on the island thought he was Penny's father.

But he had Tom's answer, and that was all he wanted.

When he told Wilbur Tom's answer two days later, aboard the sloop on the way to the fishing grounds, Wilbur's eyes grew fierce and Gardner was worried for a moment that Wilbur was going to rip loose the wheel.

"Gardner, I don't have to take that from Tom Carroll. I am going to turn that confounded girl out, and it'll be up to him to take her in or be damned."

Gardner believed Wilbur would do it, and so the first thing he did when they arrived in harbor two days later was take Tom aside and relay what Wilbur had said. Tom, jabbing his finger into Gardner's chest to emphasize every word, said, "You tell that idiot to go ahead, and if that girl dies of exposure, it'll be on his conscience, not mine."

Nothing happened for another week. Meanwhile, Tom Carroll and Wilbur Dunning took pains to be downright friendly to each other, a necessary part of this third-party-involvement-in-differences custom of island life — Winter Islanders understood their interdependence and the absolute need to look out for the welfare of one's neighbor. Wilbur went so far as to beat twenty-odd miles to the mainland against a contrary gale in icing temperatures to pick up a bottle of patent medicine which had failed to arrive on the last ferry run, for Tom, who considered the medicine necessary for his nerves. Tom went so far as to take horses into his own woodlot, get out some firewood and cut and split it for Wilbur's stove, the winter having been cold and Wilbur's frequent absences, poverty, and rum drinking having all contributed to an inadequate supply.

This difference between Wilbur and Tom was watched closely by the rest of the islanders. There was much talk among the women about poor Penny and how hard life had been for her and how hard-hearted either Wilbur was or Tom was, depending on the point of view. Everybody knew that Wilbur planned to throw her out, and they were all waiting to see if it would really happen.

Penny herself did not appear to be aware of anything out of the ordinary. However, she had stopped bringing up a chair to sit beside Wilbur at his window when he was at home.

One day in mid-March, when yet another heavy blizzard was piling up great drifts before the house and across the path, and recent hints of the arrival of spring were forgotten, Wilbur got thoroughly saturated with rum and fell from his chair into the middle of the floor. This was the first time he had passed out under the influence of drink.

Having noticed that Wilbur was not at his window, Gardner stopped in and found Penny struggling to get Wilbur into his bed. He helped her with this, and that evening stopped in again; Wilbur was still unconscious and looked sick.

"Would you like me to find a woman to stay with you?" Gardner asked Penny.

She just shook her head. He left her watching by the bedside with the lantern turned low.

In the middle of the following morning, when Gardner could next stop in, he found Penny trying to get Wilbur to lie back in the bed. Wilbur didn't seem to know who he was or where he was; he struggled and writhed until he was exhausted. Then Penny tried to get him to drink clam chowder, but as soon as she came near the bed again he renewed his struggles, fending her off.

"You know," Gardner said to his wife that evening, "it lays heavy on your heart to see Penny working so hard to get him to drink chowder or one of her teas. He fights her all the time and seems to hate her so. I'm sure she set up all last night, and I never caught her asleep today. She'll set up tonight, too, I'll bet."

The next morning, Wilbur was much improved, and he continued to improve all day; the fourth day he was on his feet, fierce and strong again.

Early the next morning, Penny was seen wading through the

drifts left by the blizzard, carrying a bundle. She went into the woods behind the village, and nobody had seen her come out by about an hour before dark. Gardner went and knocked on Wilbur's door, but got no reply. He and two other men sent by their worried wives set out on Penny's track. They found her deep in the woods, sitting huddled under the upturned root of a fallen spruce tree. She had her arms around her knees, and her chin on them, her bundle beside her. When she saw the men, she watched them with the eyes of a wild animal that has been shot.

"Shall I carry you?" Gardner asked her, as he took her by the hand and helped her to stand up. She stood, very stiffly. She was blue with cold.

But she walked. She even carried her own bundle, would not let any of the men carry it for her. Gardner took her to his house, since he felt responsible after his part in the difference between Tom and Wilbur.

His stout, firm-willed wife hustled Penny into a hot bath that had been heating on the stove ever since the men headed out. Then Mrs. Hawkins had one of her four daughters serve the evening meal, and made her husband say blessing, after which she tartly rebuked him for not asking the Lord's mercy and blessing on the poor abandoned girl Penny, and made him add this to the prayer.

On Winter Island, as in most Maine towns and villages of the time, there was a woman who grew herbs for medicinal purposes. People who had a complaint of one kind or another would go to her for something to relieve it, if their wives' own medicinals didn't seem to be doing the trick. Old Marm Jacobs, as for half a century she had been known to all on the island, lived in a small weathered house at the southern end of the village, separated from the nearest neighbor by several hundred yards and a thick wall of bushes of different kinds, which she'd planted many years previous. Old Marm had lived alone in this house since her husband died, seventy-odd years before. A few remembered him, but only dimly. He had been from away and was drowned at sea shortly after marrying and settling here. Old Marm herself was said to be an island girl, the daughter of a man who was with General Washington at Valley Forge, but this last might have been just a patriotic fable.

Old Marm Jacobs was well liked and trusted. Nearly every baby born on the island within anyone's memory she had midwifed, and most of the dead were buried in her shrouds. She was considered the authority on medical questions, and people also asked her about the movements of fish, the proper time to plant for the best crop, and a great deal else. If a question seemed to have no easy answer, you asked Old Marm.

Therefore, a few days after Penny was found in the woods, Gardner Hawkins, with a firm push from his wife, went along the path slushy with snow melting in the warm sun to the familiar opening in the wall of bushes.

Once you passed the bushes there was a definite tang in the atmosphere, though the odd-shaped little gardens surrounding the house were still under the snow. There was the smell of the sun on the spruces in the woods behind the house, but there remained somehow those other smells, too, which were to be found nowhere else on the island, except fleetingly sometimes in someone's herb closet or pantry.

The door opened to Gardner's knock almost immediately, and a short, broad, full-skirted old woman with sharp eyes the color of robins' eggs looked up at him.

"Why, Gardner," she said, in a tone that made him feel again like a small boy coming here to get tansy if one of his brothers or sisters had worms, or pennyroyal if somebody had a cold. Old Marm had a way of treating everybody on the island as children, as to her they must have seemed. "Whatever brings you along to see me?"

"Well . . ." he began, but she interrupted.

"Oh, come," she said, "don't be bashful, Gardner, come straight in."

He followed her in, feeling, in spite of himself, still awed by the curious insides of the room. The place was full of knickknacks of strange, ancient, or foreign origin, he could not tell which. And then there were the startlingly shaped bits of driftwood that looked exactly like hands, feet, faces, animals, and so on — not carved, just naturally that way.

"Sit down, sit down," she said, pointing out a chair with a colorful covering. When he sat, she went into her small kitchen adjoining and brought cups and saucers and a pot of something steaming and some small slices of cake on a platter.

As she poured, she said, "Camomile tea is such a settling thing to the nerves," and she looked him over with her sharp eyes smiling, but more sharp than smiling.

"It's always a marvel how you know what ails a body by just looking at him," Gardner said, taking the cup she handed him.

"Ah, well, it's not a hard thing," she said, and she leaned forward, hands in her lap, the cup she'd poured for herself just to be sociable still sitting in the platter. "And how is Penny doing?"

He set the cup on the low table between his chair and hers, next to the platter.

"Well, perhaps you know then about Wilbur turning her out."

"It was a heartless thing to do, but then the poor man is distraught."

"And you probably also know that Tom Carroll refuses to take responsibility for her."

She nodded gravely. "That," she said firmly, "is just as well."

"Well then, you see what the question is. What am I going to do with the girl? She rightly belongs to one or other of them, but neither will take her. She has no suitors, so she doesn't appear to be likely to solve the problem herself by getting married."

"O the laws, Gardner," she said, sitting right back in her chair and laughing. "I thought ye had a sharper wit than that. Almost anyone would give her a home." The laughter faded, leaving an expression peculiar to her, of gentle kindliness combined with an iron determination to avoid a clearly seen pitfall right ahead. She stared into space this way for a moment, and then she reached across the little table to grasp Gardner's big hand and looked earnestly and searchingly into his eyes.

"Gardner, pity can be cruel, and that girl must not be taken advantage of," she said.

Gardner looked at her, feeling confused. "I don't know as there is too much danger of that," he said doubtfully. "I think she would have been in trouble before this."

The old woman's eyes danced back and forth between his, and what was going on behind them he couldn't tell.

She patted his hand and sat back, looking off across the room.

"Well, Gardner," she said with the decisive briskness of her best bedside manner, "I think I can solve your problem for you. You send the girl along, and I will give her a home here with me. How's that?"

Late June was the time when Marm Jacobs' busy season began. She had in her gardens sweet-mary, sweet-brier, wormwood, southernwood, mint, sage, borage, thyme, balm, and the like, as well as many strange and aromatic herbs that she never divulged the names of. But there were also herbs that grew wild in various places about the island, and it was mainly these that kept her busy with gathering. On top of this she brewed spruce beer, a cool drink that she was known for among not only the islanders, but also the schoonermen who stopped at the island to buy herring for bait from the weirs. Thus, having Penny around was a help to Marm Jacobs. She could go off to gather herbs, leaving Penny to serve the spruce beer.

But on an early morning in mid-July, Marm said, "If you are ever to learn anything, you must come with me to see where to look for things. Today we shall get young Joey Hobbs to row us around to the stream by Boom Beach and land us. It's a quiet day and the boat should be able to get in and out of the stream over the bar without any trouble. I'm going to show you where the pennyroyal grows."

Penny shrank back into the kitchen doorway, her thin bare arms tightly folded, her eyes getting big and startled.

"Come, Penny, what are ye frightened of?" Marm said.

Penny was growing pale. Marm poured some spruce beer and added camomile and made Penny drink the brew. But she was not calmed by this.

"There is nothing to be frightened of on the other part of the island," Marm said, looking at Penny closely. "You must learn to speak up more often, Penny," she added. "Folks can never tell what you're thinking, and they are apt to think you don't like them, being silent all the time."

Penny, now sitting across the dining-room table from Marm, looked at the pattern of the lace cloth. "There's pennyroyal down along the path to Southern Head," she said in a low voice.

"I know there is," Marm said. "But I have already gathered all of it. We need much more. There is a place on the north end of the island just at the edge of the field above the bluffs where the best pennyroyal grows. That is where we are going."

Penny shook her head quickly and emphatically, still looking at the tablecloth.

Marm looked even more closely at her.

"It is the sea, isn't it?" she said.

Penny looked up, then down again, nodding a little.

Marm sat looking at her for a long time. Then she said, "Perhaps then it is for the best. I will go around alone."

The summer was gone and it was November. A northeaster was raging. The entire island shook under the impact of heavy seas, whose deafening roar on Boom Beach could be plainly heard even indoors in the village, over a mile away. This was the storm that threw rocks the size of big pumpkins onto the top of the eighty-foot cliff from which Almira Dunning had jumped. In the village at midday there were lamps on in many houses, and pulled near where close work was being done. Many people were down with the chills, and Marm Jacobs was doing a big business in hops bags, as well as pennyroyal and red pepper, and tansy bags for some who preferred them to hops. Penny was running here and there through the lashing rain and wind carrying these medicines and others to those who needed them.

In Tom Carroll's store, a group of island men fortunate enough not to be off somewhere at sea sat about the stove smoking their pipes or chewing their tobacco, drinking hot buttered rum, and telling each other old stories that everyone had heard many times before, nobody mentioning the storm or the men from the island who were out in it. Wilbur Dunning and Gardner Hawkins were there. Tom Carroll sat on a stool behind his counter doing some sort of figuring. His big lazy grey cat was curled up on a pile of fishnet against the wall not far from the back of the stove.

Findley Morse was telling an elaborated version of his experiences fighting Rebels down south in the Civil War, when the door opened and in with a blast of cold rain and wind came a perfect stranger.

He was a young man, perhaps not a great deal over twenty. He wore an oilskin jacket, soaking wet sailcloth pants, no hat on his head of brown hair. He stood before the door he had just shut on the weather with his head down and slightly to one side, shyly.

The men simply stared, everyone trying to imagine where this fellow could possibly have come from.

For some little time it appeared that nobody was going to do anything, and then Gardner Hawkins said, "Well, come warm yourself, friend. No point in standing way over there by the door. I reckon we could use a new log or two on that fire anyways, presumin' Tom won't mind."

Tom came around from behind his counter, still unable to take his eyes away from the stranger for astonishment. He stirred the grate and put wood on the fire. The stove roared when he shut the door. The young fellow had meanwhile come silently to stand next to the fire.

Isaiah Crocker shoved a chair towards the newcomer and said, "Don't be afeared to sit down, son."

The man sat down, and went on holding his hands to the fire.

"Why," Gardner said, "I reckon he wouldn't mind a tot of that hot buttered rum there."

The rum was poured, offered, and accepted. Then silence fell. The storm thundered and the fire roared, drawing hard. The newcomer filled the place with the fresh smell of the sea.

They waited for the young man to explain himself, but he was silent. He seemed bashful. Gardner kept opening his mouth to say something, then shutting it.

The newcomer finished the rum.

Gardner said, "Them clothes look mighty wet and uncomfortable. It might just be that Tom would have something around here that was dry, if you wanted."

This appeared to be agreeable to the young man, though he still had not spoken a word, and did not even nod yes or shake his head no to the suggestion of dry clothes. They found him some dry clothes, and he put them on and came and sat down with them again by the fire. Gardner even poured him another rum, and again they sat silently.

The young fellow seemed to be struggling with his thoughts, and then with his words, and then finally he asked, voice low and diffident, "What do you call this island?"

"It be called Winter Island," Findley Morse said promptly.

The young man nodded, and now he looked around at them all with open curiosity. As his eye lit on each man, that man felt an indefinable something which surprised him and changed his idea of the newcomer from a simple, tongue-tied, young fellow far from home to something much more, though just what none could have said.

"Do ye mind telling us your name?" Gardner asked at last.

"Oh," the newcomer said uncertainly. "My name is Anthony Stilwell."

"And how came ye to be on Winter Island?"

"My boat was wrecked," he said, sounding apologetic.

The men looked at each other.

"Did it take you long to find the village then?" Findley asked, after thinking things over a moment.

Anthony Stilwell looked at him searchingly, with the expression of one asked to figure the weather for week after next. "No," he said. "I just found the path and came in from the head straight to the village. It leads right here and it is not far."

– 26 –

The men looked at each other again.

"Were you hurt then?" Findley asked.

Anthony studied him thoroughly, glanced doubtfully at the others before answering. "No," he said.

"Well," Findley said, "I guess it may be none of my business, but would you mind telling me how come you were so long coming into the village?"

This seemed to bring even greater puzzlement to Anthony Stilwell. "But I was not long," Anthony said. "I was washed ashore and I found the path and I came straight here."

The men looked yet again at each other, incredulous expressions coming over their faces.

Gardner removed the pipe he had been earnestly and futilely sucking on without thought during the last few minutes.

"Are you saying that you were wrecked *in this storm* and you got ashore *safe and sound?*"

Now Anthony's curious gaze turned to Gardner. "That's right," he said. "And it was a shame about my boat, too. She was a fine boat. My uncle built her."

"A shame about his boat, he says," said Findley, removing his pipe to speak, then returning it to his mouth; and he looked drolly about the company. Then he removed his pipe again and hooted at the ceiling.

"Well, I should certainly *say* so," Gardner said, and he fetched his knee a whack with the flat of his hand.

There was general laughter all around, which rose and filled the store. Wilbur, whom no one had seen smile in years, cracked into one and then even chuckled, eyeing Anthony. Meanwhile, Anthony looked confused.

"And," Gardner said, when the laughter had subsided, "just look at him. I think he must have found the whole business a mite tedious, wouldn't you say, folks? Doesn't even know what's so funny."

This brought another laugh all around from men who hadn't laughed like this in quite some while. With the hard times on in the codfishing business, there hadn't been too much to laugh about.

"Young feller," Findley said, "I believe it was a lucky thing for ye that ye never noticed how them waves was piled up over fifty foot high, or maybe you would have got yourself a bruise or two and been put to some trouble, maybe, getting to shore."

More roaring laughter. Anthony was smiling uncertainly, looking a bit overwhelmed.

Finally, the laughter subsided, and the men started fussing with their corncob pipes. Anthony still seemed a bit taken aback. He sat looking into his rum, the uncertain smile fading but not yet gone.

"You don't know the heft of what you done," Gardner said to Anthony, more seriously. "Either you're just the lucky kind or you got more way with a boat in the water than anybody I ever heard tell of."

Anthony passed up the opportunity to leave on the mail boat two days after the storm, surprising everyone. Gardner had taken him in, but now Gardner's wife insisted Anthony be asked to find other quarters because there really wasn't enough room for him at their house.

"Wilbur rattles around in that house of his," she said. "I don't see why he don't take him in. It might slow down his drinking some, too. He'd have somebody to talk to when he's to home, instead of just drinking himself senseless like he does."

So now Gardner had another bit of arranging to do. He went along to see Wilbur, who happened to be down on the shore in his fish house baiting trawl lines for the next trip out. Gardner sat down to help with it, and he puzzled this way and that how to suggest to Wilbur that he take in Anthony, and also put him to work on the boat. The last thing was actually of more interest to Gardner, and was his own idea. It was his belief that Anthony was lucky. After the storm had calmed down a little, there had been a search for salvage from the wreck of Anthony's boat, and all they found were a few boards and some tangled line and a shred of sailcloth. Anthony showed where he'd come ashore, outside along the Head, and some people just wouldn't believe it, since it was all rocks there, and the waves would smash most any boat into lath and kindling in one blow on them if any sea was running at all, never mind in a storm like the one they'd just had. Anthony had said he rode a wave right up onto the shore, and when the water washed back it left the boat high and dry and he jumped out and ran for it before the next wave came in. That next sea sucked the boat back and the third one tumbled it and it came up boards out of the foam.

"That Stilwell boy wants to find a berth," Gardner said. Anthony had said very little, and had never mentioned wanting to fish, but he had spent time looking over the fishing boats in the harbor, and Gardner figured he could read that plain enough.

Wilbur glanced up. "What do you take him for?" he said.

"Well, I can't really say. But there's one thing: anybody that can ride his boat right up onto the top of the rocks and just step out on practically dry ground and walk away in a storm like that has got luck."

"You want to take him aboard of us."

"If his luck fishing is the heft of what it is on getting to shore safe and sound, we'll be millionaires."

"Not in my boat, we won't."

"Won't what?"

"Be millionaires."

"You agin having him then?"

There was a short silence. Wilbur worked at his trawl line. Gardner thought of old Zeke's comment just this morning about Anthony having used up a whole lifetime's worth of luck getting to shore that way. There had been talk like that, but Gardner thought it was just envy, mostly.

"Well, I guess if he don't leave, he'll have to go out with somebody, won't he?" Wilbur looked up and gave Gardner a pugnacious glare. Gardner was pleased. He knew Wilbur enough to know Wilbur wanted Anthony along as much as he did, only Wilbur wasn't going to admit to it.

"Well, that's settled then," Gardner said. "But the wife wants him out of the house, says he's making things too crowded." He paused. "I guess she's right, really." He paused again, studying the tie on a hook. "I guess if you were to want company you could probably have it. Course, he don't amount to much as a conversationalist."

"First you wheedle him on board of us, and now you want to wheedle him into my house."

"I'm just letting you know he won't be staying to my house, is all. It's up to you, you want to ask him to stay to your place."

"I don't need no company."

Gardner didn't say anything more about it, but he noticed later that day that Anthony was gone. And when he asked his wife where he'd gone, she said she had seen him go up to Wilbur's and he was still there.

All the gear was aboard. Gardner had gone up to his house to say goodby to his wife. Wilbur and Anthony were standing on the pebble beach where the peapod was drawn up. Anthony was looking up the beach at a heavily bundled figure watching him from the lee of Dan Thompson's fish house.

"Who is that?" he asked Wilbur.

Wilbur looked.

"That's Penny. Don't pay her any mind. She ain't right in the head. She lives with Old Marm Jacobs, delivers things around for her."

Penny and Anthony stood looking at each other without greeting or acknowledgement until Gardner came trundling down from home.

They left the island with a favoring breeze, and were on the grounds before noon. Anthony was left to cook while Gardner and Wilbur rowed off in the peapod to set some of the trawl lines. When they came back, Anthony had fish hash and molasses-sweetened coffee ready for them. After they had eaten, Anthony and Gardner went off to check the trawls and see what they were catching.

They weren't catching as much as they wanted.

Anthony was gazing with interest off to the north. He was different out here on the water, Gardner thought. As soon as they had left the beach in the peapod, he'd noticed the difference in Anthony. He no longer seemed to do everything cautiously the way he did on land. In a boat, he seemed to come alive and to know exactly what he was doing. Now he was at the oars of the peapod, but he wasn't rowing.

"What do you see?" Gardner asked him.

"We ought to set these trawls over to nor'ard a bit," he said. "The fish are mostly over there."

Gardner looked over at the sloop where Wilbur stood with a hand on a shroud, watching them.

"Well," Gardner said, "let's just move these trawls over then, and set the rest there, too."

This made a big difference. When they later pulled the trawl lines over the peapod's gunnel, about every hook had a haddock on it. They had a full boat in short order.

"I never seen such fishing around here," Gardner said to Wilbur as they pulled alongside the sloop with the first load.

Wilbur looked like he wanted to growl, but instead he just helped bring the fish aboard the sloop. They moved the sloop closer to the spot where Anthony had found the best fishing and went on pulling in the trawls.

They worked hard until midafternoon and filled their fish

holds. Fishing for haddock, for the fresh market, there was never time to fill the fish holds before heading for the mainland port where they sold the catch. Yet this time they had done it. As they set sail for port, Wilbur looked dazed. Anthony, who had worn a look of great happiness ever since leaving shore, now sat coiling line carefully back into a tub, doing it as though there were nothing else in the world he would rather do. Gardner decided that the fisherman's lot really wasn't so bad.

They sold the fish, got a good price, stayed the night in the mainland harbor, and returned to the island on the breast of a heavy gale.

There was a three-day spell of weather, and they didn't leave port. Anthony spent a lot of time hanging around outside, though it was cold and rainy and the wind was blowing hard. He kept wandering up and down the path before the houses of the village, and this caused a little talk.

Mrs. Winslow, visiting Mrs. Jameson, saw Anthony go by, and she said, "There goes that nice Stilwell boy again. I wonder what can possess him that he wanders up and down in this weather."

Mrs. Jameson leaned forward confidentially over her darning.

"It's Penny Dunning that has him out there. You know she is always delivering hops bags and suchlike for Old Marm, and he's waiting for her to come by. I saw the two of them before he went off fishing. He was standing down on the beach beside the peapod with Wilbur — they was waiting for Gardner to get down, I believe — and she was standing up side of Dan Thompson's fish house, and they was looking and looking at each other."

"So that's the way of it," said Mrs. Winslow knowingly, and they smiled at each other.

Findley Morse stepped out his back door to get an armload of firewood and happened to see Penny walk around behind his neighbor's house, her delivery bag in her arms.

"Hello, Penny," he said, a little surprised, but she ignored him and, glancing over her shoulder, continued her circuit of the house and returned to the path again.

He had just filled his arm with wood when here came Anthony Stilwell, looking this way and that.

"Hello, Anthony," Findley said, but Anthony looked at him as though he didn't understand the language and after looking around again, he went on around to the path.

Findley suddenly understood what was going on, and he chuckled, and was still chuckling when he went inside.

The second fishing trip started on the tail end of the gale, and it was very cold. This time, when they got onto the grounds, Gardner asked Anthony what he thought before Wilbur had made any decision where to anchor. Anthony, with his usual quiet glow as though he'd just discovered eternal peace, which he was never without once on the water, looked around the dirty chop and said he thought the fish were over that way; and Wilbur never let on, but just sailed the boat over and rounded up. Anthony and Wilbur took the peapod with six tubs of baited trawl and set off. Gardner was left to tend the sloop and a couple of lines from it.

It was bitter work in the cold; Wilbur, grey beard full of icicles, cussed continually. But Anthony didn't say anything, and if he was uncomfortable, he didn't show it. He appeared to be wholly intent on the fishing. His trawls came in with every single hook occupied by a fish. Wilbur's trawls, set in almost the same places as Anthony's, came in quite full, but never completely so. They unloaded the catch into the sloop's hold. Gardner had also been doing quite well. They all went below to warm up by the coal stove and have something to eat.

Then, since there was still time, they took the rest of the tubs of baited trawl out. This time Gardner and Anthony went in the peapod, leaving Wilbur fishing from the sloop, and the trawls got so full so quickly that they started taking them in as soon as they were set out. Anthony's always came in full.

They had the sloop's fish holds full in record time, and so, numbed and raw with cold, they set sail for the mainland. Wilbur was looking about as pleased as Gardner had seen him in some time. They had never done anything like as well as this before. Anthony was making an impression on Wilbur; that was a fact. Maybe the boy would cheer some of the dourness off the old rummy.

The next day, back in port on Winter Island, Gardner sat down with Wilbur in Wilbur's fish house to go over old trawl lines and make up some new, and he said to him, "Next thing, Anthony's going to want to fish for his own catch, not for a fifth share."

Wilbur looked up at Gardner. "He said that?"

"No. But it's bound to come across his mind sooner or later that he's the one catches the most fish, and he's the one knows where to go to get catches like that."

"Luck can change."

"So it can. But if we don't give him a fair shake, what anybody else would give him, there'll be plenty lining up to invite him to come fish with them for his own catch, and glad to have him find fish for them."

"I always found fish before," Wilbur muttered. "I guess I can find fish now."

Gardner chuckled. "You old goat. If a princess girl off a South Sea island sat down in front of you stark naked, you wouldn't let on she was any more attractive than a maggoty old barrel of fish bait. And then I'd find you off somewhere in the hay with her."

Wilbur gave him a look that Gardner read as partly amusement, partly annoyance, and partly acknowledgement that Gardner had hit close to the mark.

Then Wilbur turned serious, studying Gardner's face.

"How long you figure this is going to last?" he said.

"What? Anthony's luck?"

Wilbur's eyes searched Gardner's face.

"Anthony's just lucky," Gardner said. "Why, I reckon his luck'll last as long as he does."

Wilbur nodded. "All right." His gaze strayed absently out the window. Then he looked at Gardner again. "But someday his luck is going to run out. It's bound to happen. Good luck never runs forever."

"If you ask me, Anthony's luck won't break until Anthony's a mighty old man."

Wilbur turned back to his trawls, shaking his head a little. "Well, you just never can tell," he said.

The whole island population was talking now about Anthony and Penny. It was getting to be a common sight to see him dogging her tracks, and her eluding him yet watching him. Anthony was seen to corner her sometimes, and to talk earnestly to her, but she always took the first chance to slip away; it appeared that Anthony frightened her in some way. The talk was centered around the question of his luck. Most people liked Anthony, and though they envied him his success at fish finding, they were happy for him. But there were others who muttered darkly about Anthony being a little too lucky and a little too sure of himself to boot. Some even hinted at pacts with the devil or predicted a time in the not distant future when such tempting of Providence would bring disaster. These people thought that Penny was frightened for good reason, that she sensed what he was and what was going to happen to him. Since Penny seldom spoke at all, let alone about her feelings towards Anthony, and because of her sometimes strange behavior, it was easy to attribute strange powers or knowledge to her if you were so inclined.

The winter passed. Anthony had been given pay for what he fished, less only his share of the cost of running the boat. The fishing went very well, and, in spite of the dark rumblings from some, he was much asked by others to come aboard their boats; but he was loyal to Wilbur and Gardner. He spent his time ashore pursuing Penny but apparently getting nowhere with her.

They had switched from haddocking to salt codfishing again in the early spring, but now July arrived, and suddenly not far into the month, so did the mackerel.

Anthony came running up from the harbor and met Wilbur coming down with a spool of cotton wicking and a caulking wheel.

"The mackerel are running!" Anthony said eagerly.

"I don't give a damn."

Anthony halted, staring without apparent comprehension at Wilbur.

"We could fill your boat in an hour if you have a seine net," Anthony said.

"I don't give a damn if we could fill her in five minutes. There's work to be done before we start again for the grounds. Go on up to the fish house and you'll find another caulking wheel on that shelf by the window. That deck needs work all over it."

"But," Anthony said, waving an arm in the direction of the harbor, "the mackerel are running."

"I can see that as good as you," Wilbur said. "Mackerel is fickle. No good counting on them for anything. Now, you take the codfish. The codfish is always there, always regular, allowing, of course, for being a fish. Now where the hell is Gardner? You seen him?"

But Anthony had already walked off, headed for the pebble beach, where all kinds of small boats were being hastily launched to go mackerel jigging. It wasn't more than twenty-four hours before the mackerel schooners were to be seen just offshore, trailing an array of small craft — sloops and cutters, as well as the lowest form of fishing craft, known as smoke-boats, which were small, battered boats on the declining end of their careers, often old yawl-boats, with a little makeshift cud forward and carrying men whose movements were with reason watched closely.

While Wilbur went stubbornly on making ready his sloop for the grounds, Anthony went mackerel jigging with various people. He had all the fish he could catch, but he was not the only one. This was a run of mackerel such as the island had not seen in years. Gardner Hawkins had a dory he used for rowing around to the stream mouth near Boom Beach to tend his garden, and to torch herring from when they ran in the harbor. When Gardner saw the mackerel running, he couldn't resist jigging them himself, which did not please Wilbur much at all, since it left him working on his boat alone.

"We ought to fish that sloop," Gardner said to him the second day of the mackerel run. "We can fit out later."

Wilbur stood with a hand on a shroud looking out at the confusion of boats large and small that were after the mackerel. For quite a time he stood looking, and then he turned to Gardner and he said, "I ain't fishing mackerel. I'm a cod fisherman."

"Sometimes I just can't seem to make you out nohow nor noway, Wilbur. Here's the whole island awash in mackerel just begging to be taken and fill up our pockets with money, and you say you ain't going after them. It don't seem like you. Since when have you stopped taking a catch when you have a chance at it, I don't care if you are a cod fisherman? Being a cod fisherman never stopped you before. I recall a run of mackerel like this in the old days when you and I fished flat out for a week and a half. What's got into you?"

Wilbur turned sunken eyes on him. "Too much luck ain't always a good thing," he said.

"So that's what it is. Well, you can stand clear of it if you want, but I think you're a damn fool not to take good fishing when you can get it."

He turned away from Wilbur, and then turned back. "Good luck and bad luck will come your way just the same whether you do anything about them or not."

Wilbur looked glum. Finally, he drew a heavy breath and he said, "What you mean to say is, if I've got Anthony aboard, I've got Anthony aboard, and it won't do no good to pretend I don't." Wilbur glared off across the harbor. Then he turned a haggard face to Gardner. "Go get him then. Go on. Might as well meet my fate now as later."

"Mighty hard fate, putting money in your pocket," Gardner said to himself as he went off after Anthony.

When Anthony heard that Wilbur had changed his mind, he came in a hurry, and with no more ado they grabbed some barrels of salt and whatever equipment they could from wherever they could get it, and went mackerel catching.

They had an old net that Wilbur had dug out of the dim musty reaches of his fish house, and they patched this up as best they could and tried it on the mackerel. At first they didn't get much, but then Anthony fiddled with the net some, and the next try filled the net so full that Gardner thought it was going to burst before they could get it aboard. When they tripped the net on deck, they were knee deep in mackerel.

The fishing was good for three days, and then came what was known as a thick-o-fog, and all the mackerel fishers went into Round Harbor. The fog shut down in the early afternoon, and by four a fiddler who had a reputation all up and down the coast had been engaged, and a time was planned for that night in the abandoned fish factory up behind the store, the only place on the island big enough to hold a crowd. Work benches were set up along the walls, along with planks over nail kegs, buckets, and boxes.

When people began showing up after supper, they started right in eating peanuts and dates, and children took the opportunity to stuff themselves with candy. The fiddler stood on a box in the center of the floor, tuning up. The room warmed quickly with the presence of so many people, and the air grew thick with cigar and pipe smoke. Boys were bringing blue wooden buckets of lemonade over from the store, where Tom Carroll was doing a brisk business.

Almost everybody from the village and the fishing boats came. There were the roughly dressed seiners in keg boots, and there were the island girls dressed in their prettiest dresses; and there were the older folks and the children. The fiddler would call off a tune and start to play, and the floor would shake and sag under the tramp of many feet.

Anthony had by now gained quite a reputation as a fisherman and was very popular with the girls. He turned out to be nearly as good at dancing as he was at fishing, and whenever he finished dancing with one girl, there would be several more waiting hopefully to take her place. But nearly everybody noticed that, as he danced, his eye kept roving through the crowd, and nearly everybody knew who he was looking for.

Suddenly, she appeared, slipping in and along, with her back pressed against the wall, looking like a scared deer. She picked an obscure poorly lit corner, but Anthony had seen her, and when the Virginia reel was over, he made a beeline for her. She shrank back, eyes wide, fixed on his face.

He stopped a few feet away. The whole place quieted for a moment, as people watched curiously to see what was going to happen. But when the silence grew embarrassing, people tried to make out that they weren't much interested and went to talking with their neighbors.

Still, few missed seeing what happened. Anthony and Penny stood looking at each other for some time, and then Penny looked at his feet. She was pale and for a few moments it appeared uncertain whether she might faint. Then the fiddler called out, "Portland Fancy!" and started to play, and Anthony reached out and took Penny by the hand and drew her onto the dance floor.

When the dance was over, both of them looked flushed and dazed. They sat down on a bench at the back, a place not well lit, where there were already several couples.

"The fog will clear out soon," Anthony said to her softly, smiling into her eyes.

She looked back and forth from one of his eyes to the other. "How can you tell?"

"I don't know, it just will."

"I don't see how you can know."

He looked a little confused. "Well, I don't see what's so hard about it," he said. Then he said, "We can use Wilbur's peapod. He won't mind. We'll row around to the stream. The moon will be out."

She started back from him, looking frightened again.

"Not in a boat," she said. "I'm not going in a boat."

"Why, what's wrong with a boat?" he asked, bewildered.

"I'm not going in a boat," she said. "Not ever."

The fiddler had gone off to the store with some of the other men to drink rum, and now a sailor from one of the schooners began to sing a Comeallye, a sad, heart-rending song about a lumberman who lost first his love, and then his life. During it, Penny laid a hand on one of Anthony's. When the song was finished, Anthony took hold of Penny's hand and without a word led her outside and down towards the dock, to which Wilbur's peapod, along with innumerable seine dories and miscellaneous skiffs and other small boats, was tied. There were several couples out taking advantage of the privacy of the night on the dock. Penny stood on the dock, watching Anthony untie the painter. Then he reached a hand up towards her.

She stepped back, shaking her head slowly.

"See, the fog is clearing off," Anthony said. "Come on. You'll like it."

"No," she said. She backed off some more. Then suddenly she turned and ran.

Anthony stood looking after her until she disappeared. Then he jumped into the peapod, swung the thole pins up with the backs of his hands, snapping them in with a sharp tug on the lanyards, and he rowed off. He didn't come back until early morning.

When Wilbur, Gardner, and Anthony set off mackereling the following morning, Penny could be seen standing in the shadow of Dan Thompson's fish house. Anthony stood looking back at her as they sailed out of the harbor, and Gardner was startled to see that Anthony was missing his usual look of rapture. As a matter of fact, he actually looked unhappy.

Standing beside Anthony, looking back at Penny also, Gardner said, "She's a strange one, Anthony. You aren't the first to been put off by her. Never mind, they's plenty of pretty girls on this island. We grow them prettier here than about anyplace else on the coast. And from what I seen last night, I would say you can have your pick of them."

Anthony was silent for a long time, but then he finally said, sounding stricken, "She won't get in a boat at all."

Gardner glanced at him. "Well, I guess I've heard that before about her." He thought about how some said it was something she got from her father, Tom Carroll, but he didn't say that aloud. He didn't want to stir up Wilbur, for one thing, and for another, he didn't know if Anthony knew of the dispute about Penny's ancestry. If Anthony didn't know, Gardner wasn't going to be the one to tell him.

The mackerel left as suddenly as they had come, and the schooners moved on east along the coast after them, trailing a motley flotilla of smaller boats from the island and elsewhere. Wilbur and Gardner and Anthony followed for one trip, but the fish didn't seem to be schooling much now. So they finished work on the boat and put aboard more salt and cod lines and decided to tow

Gardner's dory as well as the peapod, even though it meant that Gardner's oldest son Jack would have to borrow a boat to row around to tend the gardens — it was nearly impossible to reach other parts of the island from Round Harbor overland because of the cliffs. All the while they were in harbor fitting out, Anthony was distracted by Penny haunting the shore, following wherever he went, but always staying a distance off. He made no attempt at all to talk to her. He grew a little hollow-eyed and didn't eat well or sleep well.

Finally, they hoisted sail and set off. Once they had put a day's run under the keel, Anthony seemed to perk up. After two days out, he was almost his normal self.

It was good fishing, and they wet all their salt in only about three weeks. They went out again shortly after returning, all three of them anxious to get away and not miss good fishing while it was to be had. They went a total of three trips before the weather started to turn cold. Each time they returned, Penny appeared, never smiling, never coming too close; and Anthony would look at her and would lose his appetite and much of his sleep until they were away again.

Then it was November once more.

"Time to start thinking about haddies again," Wilbur said as they came into the harbor. "We been pushing our luck pretty far, away off there on the grounds in this little boat."

"We can go one more time," Anthony said. "It'll probably be one of the best trips we'll have all year."

"You're proposing to go out there with winter coming on?" Wilbur looked Anthony over thoughtfully. "What do you think about that, Gardner? He wants to fish way off on the grounds in this little boat in the winter."

"The haddies pay well, and they are much closer to port," Gardner said.

"The cod will be biting on the banks for a few weeks yet," Anthony said.

"He's pretty sure of himself, ain't he?" Wilbur said.

Gardner shook his head slowly. "I don't know," he said. "I just don't know. I guess Anthony's likely to be right about what the cod are going to do. He seems to know more about the fishes than they know about themselves. But I ain't sure I want to chance being out there in a storm this time of year. We been pretty lucky so far this season, just some small gales. But it's gettin' mighty doggone cold now to be tending jibs out on the bowsprit with weather starting up. The last couple of trips were cold enough for me."

There was silence. Then Gardner said, "Still . . . "

"The haddies aren't doing much yet," Anthony said. "And it's not going to be a good year for them, I don't think. But this is a good cod year."

"Well, I will say that for it," Gardner agreed. "It is a good cod year. We done all right, considering everything."

"We have just about time enough left to wet down another load of salt," Anthony said. "But if you don't want to go, you don't."

They made no decision for three days, yet they got the boat ready for another codfishing trip offshore. When they talked about the question, they never let on about the getting ready they were doing, talking things over just as though they hadn't decided. Then there was nothing left to do, salt aboard and all, and finally Wilbur said, "Well, I guess I'm as ready as I'll ever be to meet my fate. And if the haddies aren't going to do much yet, we got to make it where we can. It'll be a long winter."

"Listen," Gardner said to him. "If you don't want to go, just say so."

"Didn't I just say I was ready to meet my fate?"

"If you're going out there to meet your fate, I ain't sure I want to go," Gardner said.

"Well, Anthony's our lucky boy," Wilbur said, whacking him with the flat of a big hand. "Don't you sweat, Gardner, he'll bring us home safe and sound."

"Never mind him," Gardner said to Anthony. "It's just rum talk."

So they sailed. The other islanders had things to say about this to each other, mainly that it was foolhardy. Now for the first time most talk was that maybe Anthony was a little too sure of himself, and that maybe Wilbur and Gardner had spent a little too much time listening to him and had lost their good sense. Some of this talk was just jealousy, but not all of it. More and more people were getting to think that Anthony's luck had been too good for too long, that Anthony and the men he sailed with were getting to take it too much for granted, that one day Anthony's luck was going to run out, and that like as not that day could be soon, maybe even on this trip.

Wilbur, Gardner, and Anthony fished their hold nearly full during a time of clear, cold, still weather. They had a thick-o-vapor most of the time, but they didn't worry about it since they stayed put and fished, keeping the small boats always within a short distance of the sloop, or sometimes even fishing direct from the sloop. They had no trouble finding cod. It seemed that there was cod enough to fill the whole Maine fishing fleet full to the scuppers and gunnels with plenty to spare.

Then one night the timbers and rigging began to creak. There was a long swell beginning to run, which quickly became steeper and higher when the wind started. Before long it was blowing gale force from the northeast, and a real thick-o-snow was coming down.

By this time they had broken out their anchor and were hove-to under reefed main and jumbo. They took in the jumbo soon after, as the wind force was increasing, and then they took in the main and set a heavily made trysail.

This was too much sail before morning, and so they handed the trysail and rode to a sea anchor. Then the line parted, so they started scudding under bare poles, the two small boats half full of water now trailing astern on long lines, helping to slow them down, but jerking heavily on the quarter bitts, to which they were belayed.

"Them bitts won't take much more," Gardner said worriedly. He and Wilbur were below getting warm by the coal stove while Anthony stood at the helm.

Wilbur's face was grey and his hands shook. The yellow light of the oil lantern swinging wildly in the middle of the cabin from a beam, mixed with the ghastly grey light coming through the portholes made him look even worse than he would have otherwise. He fixed Gardner with a glare.

"I knew it was going to happen sooner or later," he said. "I knew we been having more than our share of luck, and been pushing it pretty much too far. Now Anthony's luck is running out and ours with it, and we be through."

"What the hell are you talking about?" Gardner said. "We seen storms before. We'll likely see a good many more. The only thing I'm worried about is them bitts. I just don't know how much they'll stand, 'fore they rip right out. But I guess there ain't much we can do, and meantime the boats keep us headed to leeward. She ain't so likely to trip over her forefoot with them trailing out behind."

"Gardner, this storm ain't half started. The glass is only just starting to fall. And you saw how high it was to start with. I never seen it so high, I don't believe."

"Have a tot of rum. It'll warm your insides."

Wilbur glared at him, hanging onto the edge of a bunk with one hand.

"What I'm thinking is, Anthony's luck is running out and I don't want him sailing my boat. I'm sending him below, and you and me are going to do the sailing. If we ever get home alive, he's not coming with us again. His luck is turning, and ours with it."

"We need his help. You can't just send him below. There's got to be somebody at the helm all the time, and somebody pumping most of the time. You and me, we'll never last it out if we don't get a rest now and then."

"We'll last or we'll drown," Wilbur said shortly. "I ain't having *Anthony* sailing us into a watery grave."

There was no use arguing with him — Gardner knew Wilbur well enough for that.

When they went on deck, they found the storm had grown worse. Foam was flying everywhere so thick that you couldn't really tell the line between water and air anymore. Waves towered up astern, looked as though they were going to break aboard; but always the counter lifted up and over, and the wave passed roaring beneath. The driving snow thickened the flying foam and stung like bird shot. Anthony at the wheel looked, Gardner thought, as much at home as if he were rowing around the harbor on a flat calm, enjoying the day. No, not quite like that, because he looked a little excited, like a youngster with a new toy.

The boat was going faster than she should, even dragging the two boats astern, and she was sitting low in the water. Gardner was getting worried they might sail the boat right under. He'd heard stories about ships being sailed under, and he wasn't quite sure if he believed those stories or not. Could it happen to smaller boats, too? The boat sure did seem to be sitting low. In any case, this was not the best downwind boat with a heavy sea running. She always wanted to trip. Going so fast, she was getting very hard to steer, and Anthony really had to work to keep her going straight. Still, he was doing an expert job, and as far as Gardner could tell, he was enjoying it.

Wilbur stepped up to Anthony at the helm and jerked his thumb over his shoulder. Anthony seemed reluctant, but he gave the wheel over into Wilbur's hands and went below. Gardner went to work at the pump. Then he and Wilbur switched places at noon.

The wind force was still increasing, though the snow had turned to sleet and slacked off a lot. The seas were so huge that when the boat was in the trough, the sky seemed to narrow notice-ably to a band overhead. There was no chance of hearing a word, even shouted directly through cupped hands into an ear, over the roar and shriek of the wind. Ragged, airborne spume pummeled the men and boat with terrible force, while the sleet might as well have been nails flying around, it hurt so much. Still, the boat had not taken aboard too much green water.

Anthony stuck his head out of the hatch and was starting to climb out into the cockpit when Wilbur caught sight of him and emphatically jabbed with his thumb indicating Anthony was to go below again. Anthony looked surprised and puzzled, but he slowly went below again and pulled the hatch closed.

Suddenly, without any warning at all, the wind shifted from the northeast to the northwest, blowing with perhaps even greater force.

The sloop slammed over on her beam ends, green water pour-ing in over the cockpit coaming, boiling around their feet. Wilbur, at the pump, had been caught completely off guard, and he was thrown heavily across the cockpit, the coaming and deck edge stopping him by catching him across the back. The water then poured in and swirled him around and around and half out of the boat as she righted.

The jolt had torn loose the boom and gaff lashed together with the sail bundled between them, and this swung back and forth unpredictably across the cockpit, sometimes fetching up hard against one after shroud or the other. Soon one shroud parted, and then the other shroud on the same side tore loose.

The confused sea brought on by the change in wind direction tossed the little sloop wildly, without rhythm or pattern. Gardner fought with the wheel, trying to get control of the boat again.

The hatch opened and out stumbled Anthony. Wilbur lay on the cockpit floor unmoving, either dead or unconscious. Anthony glanced about, then motioned to Gardner to get Wilbur below, and he came and took the wheel from him.

Gardner had to hang on with one hand at all times to keep his footing, and so getting Wilbur below was very difficult; but in Anthony's hands the boat came back under control and started scudding off at an angle before the new wind direction, which made Gardner's struggles with Wilbur a little easier.

Wilbur was alive, but in pain from the injury to his back. He didn't say anything intelligible, just moaned and groaned. Gardner wedged him in his bunk as comfortably as he could, and then hurried back on deck.

As he stepped out into the brutal force of the storm, he happened to look at the starboard quarter. It looked somehow unnaturally empty, until he realized that the quarter bitt was missing, snapped off at deck level. Somewhere back in the storm was his dory, and fifteen fathoms of good manila line.

But considering the confused surfing sea, the sloop was riding well. Anthony pointed at the loose boom with gaff and sail lashed to it still swinging loose, and Gardner nodded.

He looked around the cockpit and reached up under the after deck where spare lines were kept in a slatted bin and got himself a length of one-inch manila. He made one end fast to the traveler, to which the broken strop of the lower sheet block was still attached. Then he waited his chance and hurled the line over the swinging boom and, at the right moment, pulled the line up and snagged it around the sheet cleat. Eventually, he got more lines around the boom and lashed it down massively to make sure it didn't get free again. Finally, he lashed the flailing loose shrouds to the mast.

Then he began to pump. The boat sat so low in the water that she was easy prey for boarding seas, which more frequently than before slopped up over the coaming and into the cockpit and drained in turn into the bilge. He worked almost frantically for quite some time — he never knew just how long — and finally sucked air.

The sea had become less confused now, as the waves came only from the northwest with the wind. The sloop cut across the huge cresting seas at an angle, so that the port quarter lifted over a wave first, and then after the boat had survived the wind-frenzied crest, the starboard bow lifted and the boat dropped down the back side. The force of the wind gave them a dangerous heel to starboard when they were being overtaken by a wave, and there was a bad moment when the quarter lifted into the full force of the wind, but the speed of the boat was much less and she was steadier on the helm. She also seemed to take on less water this way, and work at the pumps was less desperate; now it only had to be done at intervals. Anthony and Gardner spelled each other at the helm, and the man responsible for the pumps could spend part of his time below, resting.

Late in the afternoon, when Anthony had just come up from below and taken the helm from him, Gardner stumbled forward and down the hatch, muscles aching, thinking about his age.

There was Wilbur on his back in his bunk, looking at him, his face the color of ashes. And there was something else. . . .

Wilbur's greying hair had turned a startling snow white.

Gardner thought at first it must be a trick of the light, and he said nothing about it, but as he lay in his own berth, he kept looking across at Wilbur's hair. The more he looked, the more sure he was that Wilbur's hair had indeed turned white. And it had happened since the last time Gardner had taken a rest — had happened while Anthony was below.

Gardner made up his mind to say nothing to either Wilbur or Anthony about it. There was enough to think about without that.

The day passed with the wind continuing at about the same force, sometimes less. That night and the following day and the following night were more of the same, with Gardner and Anthony taking turns at the helm, pumping, and resting. Gardner kept watching Anthony to see if he had any reaction to Wilbur's white hair, but Anthony seemed the same as always. Wilbur had no mirror to look at, so Gardner supposed he didn't know what had happened.

By the end of the second full night, there was a definite slackening in the wind, and the sleet and snow, which had never really settled into one or the other, stopped altogether. The next morning dawned half clear, with slaty bits of cloud racing by overhead.

By noon, things had quieted so far that Gardner and Anthony were able to repair the damaged shrouds and sheet block and hoist a double-reefed main and jumbo and heave to. Gardner took a noon sight — a very haggard and weather-wearied man, unlike Anthony, who seemed to have thrived on the adventure — and found their position, and they all turned in and slept.

When, over a week later, they sailed into Round Harbor after off-loading at the port on the main, half the village turned out to greet them. Wilbur was still in a great deal of pain from his injury, but he was able to climb unaided from the cabin and step ashore, where he halted, stooped, to rest a moment. In the bright sunshine, Wilbur's hair shone whiter than bleached bones. There was silence among the onlookers.

Finally, old Captain Zeke said, "Well, Wilbur, blow hard enough for you?"

"Hard enough," Wilbur said wearily.

Before the day was out, everyone on the island had heard that Wilbur had turned Anthony out of his berth on the sloop. Between that and Wilbur's crippled condition and white hair, a lot of interest was aroused. Everyone wanted to know what had happened, but nobody wanted to ask Wilbur point blank, and he offered no explanations or accounts. However, Gardner was approachable, so it was not long getting out that Wilbur's hair had turned white while Anthony was below with him. Surmises were silently made, but little discussed, that Anthony was more than a witness — was a cause. There was talk about how Anthony had been the one who convinced Wilbur and Gardner to go offshore one more trip this season, and how it had been thought at the time that the three of them were getting to be just a little too sure of themselves, or as some put it, that Wilbur and Gardner were getting to be just a little too sure about Anthony's luck. Aside from those who had said all along that there was nothing but the devil in it, everybody thought that while Anthony's luck held, that was fine, but the day was bound to come when it would turn, and maybe it was starting to turn now.

The practical effect was, nobody asked Anthony aboard his boat.

Not quite a week later, Marm Jacobs opened her front door to a knock and there in the lightly falling snow was Tom Carroll.

"Why, Tom," she said. "Come in, come in, will ye?"

"Where is Penny?" he asked her, sitting down at her invitation.

She looked at him shrewdly. "Delivering. And why would ye be wanting her?"

"I just want to talk to you privately about her and that fisherman that was wrecked here. I think you should keep her away from him."

"Well, my goodness. And why should you want me to do that?"

Tom sat forward in his chair, his elbows on his knees, one hand rubbing the back of the other.

"Now, it's not that I'm her father or have any right to say what comes of her, but if that old fool of a father of hers won't take any interest, then somebody has to. Now, you been seeing to her pretty well, by all accounts, but I don't know if you know about her and that Stilwell boy."

"Well, it would be well nigh impossible to live on this island and not know about that."

"He'll go out and he won't come back one day. The way he is, it's sure to happen. Penny has had a mighty rough time already. With Stilwell, she won't have a fair chance."

For some moments, the old woman's eyes played over Tom Carroll's face. Finally, she said, "Well, Tom, that is the first sensible thing I've heard you say in years. But I'm just an old woman. I can't follow that girl everywhere she goes. I have told her that this boy is sure to go out one day and not come back, but she still keeps following him around, though I guess they aren't talking to each other much now. Maybe it will come apart by itself. We must hope so."

Wilbur had turned Anthony out of his house as well as off his boat, and Gardner had prevailed upon his wife to take him in, at least temporarily. Gardner had been shaken by Anthony's casual attitude towards the northeaster and by Wilbur's white hair and injury, and he wasn't against taking Anthony's advice with a grain of salt, but he still liked Anthony and thought him fairly harmless, in spite of the popular feeling. His wife put up a fuss, but in the end she took him in, and once having done so she wouldn't hear of his paying board until he had a place on another boat.

After Christmas, Wilbur and Gardner went off haddocking. Anthony, who had by now been around to see every fisherman on the island, without success in getting a berth, began asking where the best boat lumber was to be had, and also boat nails. He was told various things, but now more talk started, people saying that John Wilson, who owned an old sawmill and a shed and some timber on the other end of the island, should offer Anthony the use of all three. The idea was to put Anthony out of Penny's sight and reach, since Marm Jacobs reported that Penny wasn't eating regularly, and it was plain to anyone who saw her that she was wasting. There was a tendency to blame her weakness on her mother's. People said that poor Penny was not really able to deal with a lot of what she might get if she stayed stuck on Anthony. She had had a rough enough life as it was. The best thing was to get Anthony out of her sight and hope she would forget him and recover. Maybe if he intended to build a boat, he meant to sail away. He ought to be encouraged to do just that. It was hard telling what might happen to Anthony. Better if it happened far off, whatever it might be, and Penny never knew about it, had forgotten all about him by that time.

Lavinia Wilson, whose husband owned the sawmill and the old tumbledown shed by the water and the patch of timberland where grew good oak and white pine, was the one who heard the most about the solution generally thought right among the townspeople.

The pressure grew, and one day she sat her husband down and gave him a good talking to. At first he resisted, saying, "I don't see how come it's up to me to do anything just because she is pining away over some damn fool from nobody-knows-where who don't even know enough to stay close to harbor in the winter." But she kept after him until he gave in.

So it came about that on a cold, clear day in early January when the vapor wasn't very thick, Anthony stepped aboard John Wilson's little sloop, the *Mary Ann*, with some tools bought and borrowed and his few belongings in a sack over his shoulder.

Up on the bank above the pebble beach stood Penny, her face so white it blended with the snow. Anthony looked at her and she looked at him, as the little sloop bore away across the cold green winter sea. She was only a small figure indistinguishable from any of the other small figures on the shore when the sloop was about to round the northern headland at the mouth of the harbor.

Suddenly, urgently, Anthony waved to her, and she waved back.

Then they had left her behind the tall, grey, silent cliffs of the northern headland.

John Wilson showed Anthony the sawmill and the shed and helped him move in supplies and promised to be back in a week's time with a team of oxen from the mainland to help with the hauling and sawing; then he shoved off and disappeared. Anthony built a bunk in a corner of the shed, near the rusty stove, and he set up a workbench and arranged the tools. He tramped up and down the sawmill stream above the dam from which the mill got its power, picking out trees along the banks: oaks from which to get out the backbone and framing members, pine for planking and decking. He cut his chosen trees so they fell onto the ice, limbed them out, and then waited for help to arrive.

With the help of the yoke of oxen, the teamster, and John Wilson, the logs were moved to the mill. The ice was chipped to free the wheel, the saw sharpened, and the sluice gate opened. They sawed the whole thing out in two days, letting the spring-fed stream recover head during the night. It was cold but calm, and the work was warming. Towards the end of the second day, Wilson, the yoke of oxen, and the teamster left, and Anthony set to work with broadaxe, adze, and plane on five-inch flitches of oak that had been dragged into the shed.

Once every week, Wilson sailed supplies around to Anthony, and every time he left from or arrived in the harbor on these missions, Penny was there, watching. As time went by, her face got pinched, and she seemed to move more and more slowly. There got to be an eerie stillness about her.

Wilson said once to his wife, "I think it's killing that girl knowing Anthony is at the other end of the island, where she can't get to him."

"She does look poorly," his wife said. "But it's for the best."

A blizzard hit near the end of January, and the night of it, Old Marm Jacobs sat in her heavy wrap beside the fire sewing a hops bag looking towards next year's demand. Penny sat across from her, heavily bundled, but shivering slightly anyway, her pale skeletal face in shadow back in a fold of blanket. No other part of her showed. Her eyes held with a nearly unnatural steadiness to Marm's quickly working hands.

"Penny," Marm said suddenly, "I shall tell you a story. When I was a girl, not quite so old as you, a young man came here from the main. He was from Philadelphia. I fell in love with him — oh my, did I." The old woman's hands stilled in her lap and she looked for a moment into the middle distance, then abruptly she resumed her work. "He was a shipmaster," she said. "He had sailed around the Horn to the Orient several times and he had a big ship. We were married, and he built this house because he liked the island. I believed I was in heaven. And then he sailed away one day, to make another trip to the Orient, and there was a big storm and the ship was lost at sea with all hands."

Penny was very still. The blizzard shook the house.

"Penny," Marm said gently, "it's no good putting all your hopes for happiness on a seaman. Sooner or later they don't come back, and you are a widow. If you want some advice from Old Marm, you will forget about men and marriage and about happiness coming from either one, and you will learn all you can about herbs so when I am gone there will be someone here to take my place, and you will have a needful trade. This house will be yours when I am gone, so you will have a place to live — I have no one else but you to leave it to."

Penny said nothing. The fire roared in the stove, and the wind moaned in the chimney, and the snow scratched against the small dark panes of the windows.

As the winter went on, word came back with John Wilson about the progress Anthony was making on his boat. First it was heard that the keel, stem, sternpost, and horn timber were together, then that the molds were made and set up. At this point it appeared that the boat was to be a Friendship sloop. They heard shortly after that the boat was framed, and then sometime later that she was planked and ceiled up inside; and then they heard that the deck and cabin were on. It was June when John Wilson came back with word that Anthony had cut the spars and only had to rig the boat, and then he could launch. When asked what Anthony planned to do once his boat was launched, Wilson said he thought probably he would come around to the harbor and fit out. This was considered such good authority that Anthony's impending arrival became an accepted fact among the villagers, and people began watching the harbor mouth for the first appearance of the new sloop.

Penny, who had not been seen much that winter, and when seen looked sickly and as one woman put it, "not more than a tide away from death," was now to be found from dawn to dusk sitting wrapped in her blankets in a little grassy, sunny spot above the pebble beach, watching the mouth of the harbor.

Fears were voiced about what would happen to her when Anthony showed up, and there was some talk of trying to prevent his coming at all; but nothing was done. By now people were getting to be fatalistic about Penny.

Two weeks went by, and Anthony did not appear. John Wilson's wife nudged him then, and he went around to find out what was going on. When he came back, he reported that Anthony had been longer than he thought getting everything rigged and ready, but that he would probably launch the boat on the next eleven o'clock tide, four days away. He had given John Wilson the borrowed tools to return to their owners, saying that he did not think he would come back to the harbor again, but would sail straight away down east.

Penny immediately disappeared from the grassy patch from which she had been watching the harbor mouth. Some inquired about her and learned she had taken to her bed and wouldn't accept any of the elixirs or teas Marm made for her. It was said she was on her deathbed. She lay on her back staring at the ceiling with sunken eyes.

At this time of year, the sun rose out of the sea between the headlands, in view of most of the village. On the morning of the day on which Anthony intended to launch his boat, the sun's rim broke over the edge of a calm, gently swelling sea, throwing a silvery swath of light across it right into the harbor mouth. Sea birds pinwheeled, calling; a light breeze blew from the southwest. Fishermen were setting sail in the harbor.

Way out on the silver path to the sun, just beyond The Nubbin in the harbor mouth, there was a small boat under sail, heading east.

"Who's that, do you s'pose?" Elliot King asked Dan Thompson, as they both prepared to set sail for the outer ledges to tend their gangs of lobster pots.

Dan squinted at the little spritsail. "Why, it looks like Cap'n Dunning's peapod."

"I know for a fact it ain't Wilbur out there. I just seen him down to his fish house, mending cod lines."

"Well, maybe it ain't his peapod then." Dan looked over towards the dock where Wilbur's peapod was always tied up. "But his ain't to the dock."

They both studied the boat.

"I can't rightly figure it out," Dan Thompson said.

The first man to see who it was was Findley Morse, out getting an early start tending his pots.

"Penny," he said softly to himself, staring, not knowing what to make of it. She was hunched down in the boat, ignoring him and everybody else, looking where she was headed, which was now north along the seaward side of the island.

Findley's pots were right along the way she was heading, and he started pulling them, watching her, and wondering at her. As far as he knew, she hadn't been in a boat since she was a very small girl. She was doing all right for a rank beginner. It promised to be a beautiful summery day, with no chop to speak of and only an easy rolling swell that washed the sunny rocks where the seals liked to pull out and the cormorants and gulls congregated. It was pretty plain where she was headed, and since his traps were spread almost all the way to the north end of the island along this shore, he decided he wouldn't interfere with her, just keep an eye on her in case she got into trouble.

The sun rose higher, and the cliffs where the sea birds nested rang with their calls. Some other Round Harbor men had traps along here, too, and the little fleet moved slowly along in the wake of the peapod. At intervals the men had conversation about Penny.

"Mighty spunky young lady, that one is," Dan Thompson said to Findley, "considering how afraid she always was of the water."

"I guess she ain't got island blood in her for nothing," Findley returned, as his sloop drifted, boom sagging like a broken wing while he tended a trap.

By half past nine, Penny was rounding the end of the island. The fitful light wind had drifted them that distance slowly, but now the wind was picking up again, and the peapod slid along smartly, close hauled, a little white curl of water turning away from the bow.

The men in their sloops had been skipping a lot of their traps to keep up with her, and though nobody had any traps beyond the northeast corner of the island, not one man failed to follow her, at a distance, to the place of launching. All were curious to see Anthony's boat and to see how the launching would go; and there was also a feeling that no matter what you might say about Anthony and Providence, it wouldn't be proper for a Winter Island boat launching to go unattended.

Penny rowed the peapod up under the lee of the island and sent the bow onto the tiny bit of beach next to the shed where Anthony had built his boat. The boat now sat before the shed, rigged, sails bent, ready for the top of the tide. Penny stumbled out of the peapod, and at that moment Anthony appeared in the door of the shed.

The two of them just looked at each other. After a few moments, Anthony walked down to her, and they had some conversation. Then he took her by the hand, and they disappeared into the woods.

The north end of the island is an odd collection of bluffs of different heights, and cuts up into the island between them that lift only gradually from sea level. Two of these cuts are salt marshes for some distance inland, and the third begins as a kind of small, wedge-shaped cove which narrows until it becomes a stream, the tide running in as far as the series of little waterfalls. Just inside this cove stood the shed in which Anthony Stilwell built his boat. The woods were thick right to the shore here, but way up on the top of the nearest hill the woods had been cleared away many years ago, and it was there, silhouetted against the clear blue sky, that Anthony and Penny next appeared to the men in the sloops.

The sloops had all dropped anchor in the fairly narrow sound between Winter Island and the uninhabited neighboring island to the north. The men fiddled around pretending to be busy, but keeping their eyes on the pair way up on the hilltop.

They stayed up there until by Findley's reckoning high tide wasn't fifteen minutes away. He glanced up at them, consulted his watch, glanced again — and they were nowhere in sight.

Some of the men went ashore, with the idea of lending a hand, Findley Morse among them. Dan Thompson's son had a peapod which he was using to tend a gang of pots, and they all piled into that to get ashore.

As they stood around the boat on the ways, waiting, Dan Thompson ran his hand along the planking, smiling.

"He sure has an eye for a fair curve," he said. "Ain't this a fine little boat? I wouldn't mind having one this pretty."

"You notice how he tapered down that toe rail at the ends," Elliot King said. "That's professional work. I think this ain't the first boat he's built."

All the men had noticed, but none commented on, the words painted in blue on the white transom:

PENNY
ROUND HARBOR, ME.

There was a crackling of twigs, and here came Anthony and Penny, hand in hand, and both looking startlingly happy. More striking yet was how healthy Penny looked.

"The boat is ready," Anthony said, grinning around at them all. He was twirling a daisy in the fingers of one hand.

"You'd ought to be aboard of her when she goes in," Findley said. "We'll launch her."

Anthony said, "Here, Penny, I'll help you up." Then, as she moved towards the boat, he looked at the daisy in his hand and he said, "No, wait. Come back here." He put the daisy in her hair. She looked with clear earnest eyes up into his face.

He helped her up over the side and swung nimbly up himself.

"Just saw off those boards," Anthony said. "I've cut them most of the way through already. There are my two crosscut saws lying on the ground — do you see them?"

A pair of men turned to and cut the boards. One snapped and the weight thrown on the other snapped it also, and the boat slid smoothly down into the water, Penny hanging on tightly and laughing in delight, and Anthony beaming all over.

The boat floated high, bobbing a little, and Anthony picked up a sweep oar and maneuvered her over against the very dilapidated remnants of the dock, along which he had laid some new planks and piled a quantity of smooth, rounded stones from along the shore. With help from some of the men, Anthony carefully loaded the stones into the bilge until the boat sat evenly on her lines.

– 53 –

"She's a pretty little boat," Dan Thompson said. "I think she's going to be fast."

Anthony went ashore once more to make sure he had left nothing behind and then returned in Wilbur's peapod, which he tied to one of the sloop's quarter bitts. Penny sat all the while in the cockpit, hands tightly knotted in her lap, her eyes full of both excitement and fear.

Anthony cast off and let the boat drift from the dock while he hoisted sail. When he sheeted in, the *Penny* started moving at once.

"Aw, now, ain't that just about the prettiest sight," Dan Thompson said amid approving murmurs from the others.

"She is going to be fast," Elliot King said. "And weatherly, too, I'll wager."

Marm Jacobs gathered her skirts and came from the far corner of her garden when Penny came trotting through the space in the hedge.

"You look fresh as the sea breeze," Marm said, noting the daisy in the girl's hair. She had seen Penny arrive on Anthony's new sloop.

Penny laughed gaily.

"Well, tell me, and how does the little sloop sail?"

"Oh, she sails very well, Marm," Penny said, all bright and merry. "Anthony is going to go fishing, and when he comes back he will have enough money to pay the minister, and we are going to get married and live in a little house in the village."

Marm smiled at her, but with her peculiar attitude of one seeing a pitfall just ahead.

"Are ye sure now that Anthony loves you?" she asked.

"Yes."

"And that ye love him?"

"Yes."

"Well, ye two will have need of that love."

Anthony was in port for about a week, getting together fishing gear and supplies. There was plenty of talk about the marriage plans. Some said it was for the best, but there were plenty of conversations like the one between Mrs. Brackett and Mrs. Jameson.

"If you ask me," Mrs. Brackett said, "that Stilwell boy is going to break her heart one day. He will go out and he won't come back. She'll be a widow sooner or later. I just hope it doesn't upset her so much she ends up like her mother. Poor Almira was not a strong woman, you know."

The two women looked at each other with a mutual understanding of the deeper meanings of the last statement.

"Of course," said Mrs. Jameson, "she was from away. You know, Tavy, I have often wondered about Anthony. He is such a nice boy, and they say he is a fine fisherman. What can possess such a fine boy to be so foolhardy, that's what I want to know."

"What *I* would like to know is just exactly what happened out there on Wilbur's boat. I told my George, I said, George, I don't know what happened out there on that boat, but whatever it was it happened because of Anthony being aboard. I told him, I said, you're not going to even think about taking him on board your boat. I told him I didn't plan to be a widow that soon. He said I ought to quit fretting myself because he didn't have no plans along that line. He said he thought Anthony was a nice boy, and that he was about the best fish finder there ever was on Winter Island, but he said looking at Wilbur's white hair and crippled-up back was as close as he wanted to get to having the boy aboard *his* boat."

"What do you suppose happened out there, Tavy? I just can't *imagine* it. Anthony's *such* a nice quiet boy. It just seems impossible that he could have done anything to turn poor Wilbur's hair white."

"Well, a Jonah don't have to *do* anything, far as that goes; that's the unholy way of the thing. But I'll tell you something: If Penny was my daughter, I would as soon drown her as marry her off to Anthony Stilwell."

Anthony set sail with the first breeze of a beautiful morning on an ebb tide. Penny waved from the dock, and watched him out of sight. Then she walked slowly up the path to go herb gathering with Marm.

That night the house suddenly gave a creak, and there came a moaning under the eaves. Marm Jacobs awoke to find Penny already sitting up in the living room with a lantern lit. Rain was lashing the windows.

"Sou'wester," Marm said, and she sat down on the other side of the lamp and took up her sewing.

Nothing more was said for a long while. Meanwhile, the storm increased, buffeting the house, making the lantern flicker.

After arriving with Anthony in the sloop in Round Harbor, Penny had kept a vase of fresh and perfect daisies in the sunny south window of Marm's living room. Suddenly, the vase fell over and smashed on the floor.

Penny started, hands bunching at her throat.

Marm closed her eyes and bowed her old head.

"Oh, Penny, my poor dear," she said. "It has happened."

Penny's hands dropped from her throat and she grew very still, as though listening intently.

Suddenly she scrambled to her feet.

"I have to go," she said urgently. "Can I bring this lantern?" She was already hurrying to put on waterproof coat and boots.

Marm Jacobs' old heart was beginning to beat very fast and she felt faint. "You must get hold of yourself, Penny," she said breathlessly. "You have no business going out into that storm."

"Can I take the lantern?" Penny said, coming to the side of Marm's chair. "I'll light you another then," she said, and scurried to the closet where a spare was kept.

"No, no," Marm said weakly. "Go ahead, take the lantern. I'll light the other if I want it."

"Oh, thank you, Marm," Penny said, and she plunged out into the wind and rain.

Much later in the night, Mrs. Hawkins awakened when her husband became restless in the bed. She got out of bed and went downstairs, where from her kitchen window she saw a flicker of light out in the harbor.

"Gardner?" she said, going back upstairs. "Gardner?"

"Hmmm, what?"

"I think there's a ship gone up on The Nubbin."

"A ship?"

"Well, there's a light out there."

"Huh. I guess I ought to go see."

"You want to take some men with you."

"I plan to."

He roused Wilbur Dunning, Findley Morse, Dan Thompson, Elliot King, and one or two others, and they all walked out the path onto Southern Head.

They stopped at the edge of the eighty-foot cliff overlooking the harbor mouth.

The islet called The Nubbin is a rounded back of ledge about twenty yards off and to the northwest of Southern Head in the harbor mouth; on top of it is a round patch of grass partly enclosed with bushes, like a big bird's nest. The men looked down on it from the cliff top and saw a light.

"How in tarnation," Findley started to say, but didn't finish, not that anyone could hear him anyway over the storm.

Holding the lantern as high as she could, Penny stood in the little grassy patch on top of The Nubbin, wreathed in her lantern's glow, the huge seas washing occasionally around her feet.

The men looked in disbelief.

"How'd she get out there?" Dan Thompson shouted into Gardner's ear, but all Gardner could do was shrug.

Wilbur stood leaning into the wind, his big fists down at his sides, looking as old as he ever had.

"She'll be washed away, the first big wave," Findley shouted.

But there was nothing they could do. They tried yelling to Penny, but she didn't appear to hear, not surprisingly. It was too far to throw a rope in the roaring crosswind, and too rough to try to land in any sort of boat on that ledge.

So the men stood watching, waiting for the inevitable.

Then the lantern went out. They waited some more, peering through the dark and the rain, but the light did not reappear.

There was nothing more to see. There was nothing more to do. The men turned away and went silently home.

Anthony Stilwell was never seen or heard from again. No wreckage or flotsam was ever found. Penny was never seen again, nor did her body wash up anywhere, or any of her clothing, or the lantern.

Some time afterward, several people in the village became fond of telling how they had seen the light move slowly out to sea, and then flicker and fade away. These people, and those who believed them, hadn't a great deal of interest in how Penny managed to get onto The Nubbin, but there were a number of theories put forth by others. One explanation involves a bit of easier shore just inside the cliff, low tide, and the momentary draining of the shallows between the shore and The Nubbin by the backwash of a big wave. Another theory holds that Penny jumped from the cliff and was thrown up on The Nubbin by the sea; but this seems not to allow for the presence of the lantern. The fact is, no one really knows how she got out there.

Two days after the storm, when the water had quieted enough, Gardner Hawkins and Findley Morse rowed out to The Nubbin, stepped off on it, and took a look around. When they were afterwards asked what they'd found, Findley said, "Nothin' much. But you never saw so many daisies."

It is not known if daisies had ever been noticed there before; but ever since, anyone launching a boat, getting married, or awaiting the return of some vessel away at sea is likely to watch for a calm day to row out to pick "Penny's daisies" to bring a little of "Anthony's luck," though no one doing so will allow as how there is anything more to it than custom.   *– End*

Part Two

THE SISTERS' SONG

he Brothers had be-
gun to grow roiling white beards, and the Caldron had begun to
rumble below the tiny driftwood house perched upon its lip, and the
wind had backed into the northeast; but it was the first note of The
Sisters' song heard on The Devil's Island that brought the tattered
figure bursting forth from the house to fly this way and that over the
island's barren, knobby hills.

It was late in the day, the slaty sky hung low over the treeless
island, and colors were faded to black and grey. The island's sole
inhabitant, with his tangled wreath of beard and ragged sea coat,
blended in so well he was invisible when motionless. When he
moved it was with nearly unnatural ease and speed over the rough,
brushy terrain, like a nervous deer. He would bound along to a
vantage point overlooking the half-mile-wide passage between The
Devil's Island and The Brothers and The Sisters and peer intently off
into the stiffening breeze, then suddenly bound away to another
vantage and again examine the horizon. In his hand he carried a
fine old brass spyglass, and frequently he would bring it to his eye
and swing it about the horizon, studying the distance with meticu-
lous care.

When dusk became nightfall, he was still in the open, and the driftwood house's crooked little windows — transom lights from a wreck of three years previous — remained dark. No light showed anywhere on The Devil's Island that night. Though it began to sleet not too long after dark, and the wind increased in strength most of the night, the inhabitant remained out in the open. The sea roared against the shores and soaked the seaward wall of the driftwood house with spray rising sixty feet from the depths of the Caldron. Above the roar continued the peculiar song of The Sisters, a sound not heard on the island except when the sea was at her most treacherous.

Very late in the night, there appeared a light off The Sisters, dimly visible when the rain and sleet slacked off. When he sighted it, the man leaped up atop the rock he had previously been crouched behind and peered eagerly through his captain's glass.

"Haha!" he said. "Haha haha!" And he smacked his lips and made other sounds to himself. Then he darted away to a place on higher ground and looked again, nodding to himself, muttering unintelligibly, half speaking his words aloud.

The light, going up and down, disappearing frequently, moved in a southeasterly direction, towards The Brothers. The man ashore followed its progress eagerly, sometimes through the glass, some-times not. As the light neared the bearing of The Brothers, his muttering increased.

The light went out. The man whipped the spyglass to his eye and peered intently through it. Then he let the glass drop down to arm's length, a helpless gesture. He turned his head, listening. If there were screams from the drowning they were camouflaged by the wild song of The Sisters.

Near daylight, the wind shifted into the northwest, the storm blowing itself away to sea. Dawn was grey, and the sea ran high, sending up tall plumes here and there along the steep rocky shore of The Devil's Island, the rote deep and thundering. But though the water broke and churned among the ledges fearsomely, and The Brothers' white beards were grown broad and full, The Sisters' song was not to be heard. There was nothing to be seen at sea.

The man had gone into the house not long before dawn, but now he emerged, stealthily. He carried a stout belaying pin in his right hand and an empty burlap sack in the other. After a careful look all around, he took a steep well-worn path down to the shore.

Here he stopped well above the reach of the great waves,

crouched, watching them with unblinking eyes. When he started along the shore, he moved with the low, tight watchfulness of a wary cat.

"Ah!" he exclaimed suddenly, and darted nimbly up and down over several of the infinite number of long fingers of rock that all slanted steeply into the sea and up which the great waves raced and fell back. He dropped the belaying pin and sack and began tugging frantically at a tangle of rope which was snarled around a broken length of spar wedged between the rocks. He was not finished with that when he spied something tumbling in the surf on a tiny bit of sand beach further on — a keg, empty as it turned out. But he snatched it from the waters, darting away up the beach with it, the next wave at his heels. He ran as though for his life, in terror of even the spray sent up by the last splash of the spent wave against a round bit of granite. He eagerly looked his treasure all over, then cached it secretly far up out of reach of the water, having looked carefully all around as though to be sure he was unobserved. Then he went on along the shore. Every time he spied something he would give a cry and race for the thing as though it were the most important treasure of them all.

He went on in this way for nearly an hour and had salvaged a great number of broken planks, bits of line and rope and cable, some more kegs containing little but salt water, and a miscellany of similar items — nothing of great value — when he leaped atop yet another rock and halted suddenly.

After a moment, he put down his sack with a slight clink of empty bottles, and with his belaying pin held high he went down behind the rock stealthily.

A few seconds passed. Suddenly he leaped back atop the rock and looked all around as though in a fright. He went bounding from rock to rock to a higher vantage point and thoroughly studied the sea and the shore in both directions, as well as the acres of low scrubby bushes that made a grey haze of the slight hill behind the shore. Finally, cautiously, he went back down behind the rock, and a few moments later emerged carrying in his arms the body of a woman. He went bounding along the shore from rock to rock with apparently effortless ease, the woman's torn and sea-damp dress streaming behind.

The woman was alive, but sick. He placed her in his own bunk built against the south wall of the tiny, one-room house, piled all the old salvaged sea blankets he had upon her, heated water and made her drink a tea brewed from leaves of a wild herb. It was a very strong and bitter tea and made her cough and sputter. Her breathing was thick and she seemed only dimly conscious of her surroundings.

That night was bad for her. Her shivering fits were violent and she began to run a fever and had trouble breathing. But the next day the fever left her and the shivering spells stopped and she slept. During this time he never went out of the house except to get driftwood for the fire. When she finally slept peacefully, he sat and stared and stared, fascinated. The woman was finely made, with delicate features and graceful proportions.

After a long time, he got up and went outside and around the building to stand on the lip of the Caldron. Cautiously, he peered over the edge, looking only for a moment; the green, foam-topped sea swirled and sloshed in a mesmeric way, dangerous to one's sense of balance. Swirled and sloshed it did, and rose and fell, rose and fell.

He went down to the shore and along to a point only just above the waters of the Caldron, where the surrounding rock walls were dark with spray but there was a place to stand where the sea's greedy, grasping hand did not for the moment reach. A sea roared in through the narrow opening and the weed skirt along the dank rock lifted and flowed like coarse hair on a corpse; then as the water sucked down, the thick dark weed hung dripping, glistening a little, and below it appeared the white roughness of barnacles on sheer rock that continued straight down no one could see how far. Rising and falling. Rising and falling.

He backed away, and suddenly was gone up the steep climb to the house. He burst through the door, halted at the sight of the woman still lying peacefully asleep in the bed, and then sat very quietly in the chair by the bedside. Looking at her, his eyes grew moist, and several times he reached out to touch her gently, seeming more full of wonder and awe each time he did so.

Towards evening she awoke and moved in the bed slightly. When she caught sight of him she started and a little cry escaped her.

Her glance went uncertainly about the crowded room. The firelight danced eerily over strange old books, deadeyes, coils of rope, folded pieces of sailcloth, various sea chests, barrels of provisions — salt beef, salt cod, sea biscuit, dried apples, dried figs, etc. Hanging on hooks were bits of iron, coiled fishline, and tools. On shelves were stores of marmalade, sweetmeats, sugar, flour, bottles of rum and divers wines. And there was a great deal more, including some stray pieces of crystal and china, navigation instruments, and salt-stained charts.

He gave her food to eat and more tea to drink, and she slept again. He crept out and, belaying pin in hand, went craftily along the entire shore of The Devil's Island by the light of the stars and the nearly full moon. He found three bodies, which he investigated: that was all.

The woman awoke when he returned towards morning. She was on her feet that day. He gave her some old seamen's clothes to wear.

He went salvaging and she sat upon a rock and watched him. He pounced upon bits of broken plank from the wreck and stacked his treasures in a pile near her. Seeing the wreckage, she wept. That evening she ate little.

He slept on the floor, as she had use of the bunk, and this night, when the rising moon shone through the window upon him, he suddenly sprang to his feet and went stumbling amongst the heaps of salvaged goods until he found his belaying pin. Then he crouched with it held up ready to strike, and appeared to be listening. After a few moments without a sound but the low moan of the wind under the eaves, he began to creep about craftily until his foot touched a bolt of sailcloth on the floor in the corner; and he gave a yell and began to beat the bolt with his belaying pin. The woman screamed and pressed back into the corner of the bunk, clutching two fistfuls of blanket to her throat.

At her scream he dropped the belaying pin and leaped for her. She struck at him wildly, but he took her gently in his arms and cooed to her as though she were a frightened child.

The next morning she watched him at his scavenging unblinkingly, perched on a rock like an alert bird. By midmorning she had disappeared.

That morning had dawned grey, and there was an ominous heaviness in the rote. By late morning the wind had gone into the northeast again and spray blew from the tops of the cresting waves.

At midday he went back to the house, but she was not there. Outside the house, he stood still, poised, as though listening to an inward voice. Suddenly he made an inarticulate sound and shot across the island towards a certain secluded place on the western shore. . . .

With the help of rollers, she had managed to move the boat some yards towards the steep little pebble beach. When she saw him, she ran around to the far side of the boat and took such a hold on its gunwale that her knuckles turned white. He bounded over the boat and clasped her in his arms, burying his face in her neck; and then he hurried her off over the exposed hills into the teeth of the rising gale, now full of the song of The Sisters.

He put her in the house, and seeing to it she had no way to make a light, but did have something to eat and blankets with which to keep warm, he propped shut the door with a heavy length of broken ship timber. He leaned a moment against the wall of the house, briefly closing his eyes, then darted away, spyglass in hand.

During the night The Sisters' song became a shriek. It blew so hard he finally had to lie down behind a rock and stay there. The rote was so deafening he covered his ears, the sleet so hard-driven he closed his eyes.

In the morning he struggled to the top of a hill, and what he saw beyond brought him to his knees. The Caldron hurled forth towering columns of spray which partly obscured the view, but there was no doubt that his house was gone.

By the time the hermit of The Devil's Island died in 1910 at the age of ninety-five, mariners had come to rely on the beacon fire he unfailingly lit atop the highest hill whenever The Sisters sang of the treachery of the sea.   – *End*

Part Three

THE LAST OF THE COASTERMEN

n one of the first really warm spring days of 1905, at around three in the afternoon, the 124-ton schooner *Harraseeket* emerged from Fox Islands Thorofare bound for Rockland on the west shore of Penobscot Bay. The *Harraseeket* had a steady fifteen-knot breeze on the port beam, and the long, deep swell lifted and lowered her in slow majesty. Cloud shadows moved over the woods, fields, and buildings on the islands aft, and ahead were the hills of the west shore, blue in the distance.

Captain Leland Wells stood at the wheel, the sleeves of his worn cotton shirt rolled up, one broad hand on a spoke, a decrepit felt hat square on his head. He was about forty, of fairly average size and proportion, perhaps a bit on the sturdy side. The noticeable thing about him was the fierce brilliance of his eyes. They were as hard to look into as the sun-glint off the bay — except when he went ashore, at which time they went grey and dull and took on a fatalistic expression.

When he was at sea, neither his eyes nor his ears missed much, yet if he had lost both those faculties he would still have known much of what was happening aboard his schooner just by standing on her deck. You might say he was married to his schooner, though the relationship was very one-sided and dominated by everything Leland was, was not, believed, and didn't believe. The *Harraseeket* amounted to his wife, family, and whole life, as well as his living. He neither had anything else nor wanted anything else. He had overseen the building of her and had driven her many thousands of trunnels himself. He knew she was sound, and when it blew he never feared for his vessel. Another man might have done some soul-searching when the weather got rough, things he'd done less than perfectly and thought good enough at the time coming back to haunt. But Leland was not that kind. His attitude was that since he'd done it himself, he could count on it. It was only things other people did that he ever had doubts about. And about those things he had almost nothing *but* doubts.

Nearly twelve years of working the *Harraseeket* in all kinds of weather in all seasons — including 1898's famed "*Portland* Breeze" — had proved him justified in his confidence in himself, but Leland never thought of it that way, since there had been no doubt in his mind from the beginning.

Right now, Leland was considering what might be behind the behavior of Frank Chase, the deckhand, this past couple of weeks since they'd been in Portland last. Frank had been kind of smiley and absent, and it was wearing on Leland the way Frank didn't always seem to be paying attention.

Frank sat on the winged-out deckload of oak flitches supposedly helping to keep an eye out ahead, since Leland at the wheel could only just see over the load. But Frank was sitting turned around facing aft, letting his feet swing to the roll of the vessel, chewing on a strip of slack-salted pollock, and gazing back at the play of light and shadow on the islands.

"I like this short-haul work to Rockland," Leland said. "Never pass Portland at all."

Frank stopped chewing with his jaw down and his mouth slightly open, looking around as though he'd just awakened and didn't know where he was.

"I don't care for all these oak flitches, Cap'n," he said. "Tears my hands all up."

"Good for 'em. Toughen 'em up."

Frank didn't say anything for a little, but Leland noticed that Frank's face was contorted into an attitude of thought, which activity always seemed a hard chance for him.

"You plan to just keep on finding short-haul work to Rockland, Cap'n?" Frank asked after some moments.

"You got an objection to that, Frank?"

Frank went into deep struggles with thought. He didn't answer right away. They went to leeward of another two-master that was headed for the Thorofare. The helmsman waved and Leland raised a hand in return.

"Cap'n," Frank said finally, "I got me a girl in Portland."

"Oh ho. Is that so. And who would this girlie be?"

Frank seemed to brighten up all over.

"Susanna, to Clara Hastins'. Only she ain't to Clara's no more on account of she promised me she'd leave."

"Susanna is it then." Leland and the waters of Penobscot Bay glared at each other.

"Yes, Cap'n," Frank said, now grinning all over. He was a freckle-faced eighteen-year-old from a little gunkhole cove way down east. His father and grandfather had been deepwater sailors. Now his father just worked a little saltwater farm — like as not, Leland figured, hauled up to rot away ashore by Frank's mother.

"Let me ask you something, Frank," Leland said.

"Sure, Cap'n," Frank said expansively, still grinning.

"You want to be hauled up for good?"

Frank frowned. "You mean not go in schooners?"

"That's right. Never set foot in another schooner as long as you live. No more breaking out your anchor and heading for open water with a fair wind. No more setting up there in the fore-tops'l when it ain't flyin' and just taking the day like a seabird wheeling round and round up over the water the way you like to do. No more setting all the sail in the lockers and the cap'n's handkerchief besides and watching her walk away from some big fast three-master with a dude captain who thinks he's going to show you something."

Frank's open face reflected the work of his vivid imagination as he pictured every detail of the things Leland was waxing eloquent about.

"Be done with all that and go ashore and *stay* there," Leland said, spitting out his disgust at the very idea of anybody actually doing such a thing.

Frank looked appalled. His mouth fell wide open and stayed that way while his eyes searched Leland's for some ray of hope somewhere.

"That's what'll happen if you let a woman get hold of you," Leland said grimly.

This gave Frank plenty to think about for the time it took to sail into Rockland Harbor and up to the Maine Central pier and dock along its north side. When they had their lines out, Frank finally made a reply to Leland.

"Naw," he said. "Susanna wouldn't do that. She knows I go in schooners."

On the other side of the pier were some summer people who had arrived by train and were waiting for one or another of the bay steamers to take them out to one of the islands or to some remote town down east. Several fashionable ladies and some distinguished-looking gentlemen had come across to watch the schooners loading and off-loading along the freight side of the pier.

"Aren't they such dirty old boats!" exclaimed one pinch-faced woman.

"Now," said Leland to Frank, making no effort to lower his voice, "*that* is just like a woman. She knows nothing about anything. She can look at the handsomest schooner betwixt Cape Cod and Eastport and can't tell her from some run-out old kiln-wooder that floats into port on her cargo half the time. That's all a woman can think about anyway — whether something is dirty or old. If it ain't brand new from Paris or New York or some such place, it ain't any good."

"Well, I never," the woman said in a surprised and indignant tone. One of the gentlemen, tall and handsome with an imposing sweep of white hair and whiskers, stepped nearer and opened his mouth as though to speak. Leland didn't give him a chance. He reached down with one hand and yanked up a green oak flitch twelve feet long, two inches thick, and as much as twelve inches wide towards one end, and he hove it onto the pier one-handed, the spikes that had held it in place on top of the load flashing as the board flipped over and over in the sun until it landed. The fashionable folk scattered, with some squealing from the women.

"Stand clear ashore," Leland bellowed in a flat tone. "We're off-loadin'."

Frank stood at the main rigging looking embarrassed.

The oak flitches were ship timber headed for some yard or other where a biggish vessel was under construction. There was nothing under two inches thick, and a lot of the approximately ninety thousand board feet was six- and eight-inch stock, some of it having quite a bit of sweep to it. Unloading this thick stuff was hard work; by the time they were finished several days later, with Leland pushing hard the whole time, Frank was about done in.

Though some schooner captains would have worked only over the top of the tide, it was typical of Leland to save every minute he could when loading or unloading, and he unloaded while there was light, regardless of the long heaves at low tide. He was never in a good mood while tied to a dock. He was known everywhere as a driver, and there was sometimes speculation about what he was saving up for. He had a reputation as a sharp trader and, as far as anybody knew, spent money only to keep the schooner in good shape and for essentials. And it was generally agreed that the *Harraseeket* had to be making more money than most, since she was seldom seen going light and nobody could recall ever seeing her laid up except in the worst months of winter — which time Leland spent doing repairs.

When they moved out to anchor on the day they finished unloading, it was getting towards dark. All Frank wanted to do was get into his bunk, but Leland was still going strong and had other ideas.

"That's Dan Procter in the *Sarah* over to windward of us," Leland said as they sat at supper — Leland cooked because Frank simply could not, however he tried. "I think we'll have a little gam along o' him tonight. Dan was mate in the old *Eustace*, years ago when I was a boy. I went in the *Eustace* with him about five years, mostly hauling lumber from the Bangor River. Dan and me, we had times, I can tell you. There weren't hardly a better sailor on the whole coast than what he was. And didn't he know the Bangor River. Them days you'd see nothing but sails on that river, and not hardly a marker to steer by, no good place to anchor if the wind quit, and then there were the steamers and the tows. They was supposed to look out for you, of course, but they never did nothing but take the main channel and you'd best sail out'n *their* way and not try to be no sea lawyer. Dan, it never bothered him. The old man would say, 'Kin you take'r up, Dan?' and then he'd go below to his bunk and Dan and me would run the old *Eustace* right to Bangor without the old man showing his nose. Dan was quite a sailor, them days. He showed me most everything I know. Made a sailor out of me, much as I am anyway. But that ain't the end of the story."

Leland wiped his mouth on his sleeve, took another sip of

coffee and fixed Frank with a piercing gaze. Frank sat slack in his chair, mouth sagging open, his eyelids fluttering.

Leland's fist came down on the table, making the plates jump. Frank started awake.

"Dan was ruined by a woman," Leland said. "He got married and left the *Eustace*. The old man give me the mate's berth, and then, pretty soon after, I got a command of my own, and not too long after that I built the *Harraseeket*. But Dan, he bought that old schooner of his and been in her ever since. That old *Sarah* never made any money — that's how he got her cheap — and now he's got a pretty good dreen on his wallet all the time with that wife of his, and a daughter too. But you know the worst of it?"

Frank was drifting off to sleep again, his chin descending towards his chest. Leland glared at him, then got up and reached for the coffeepot on the stove.

Pouring Frank's cup full, he said, "Drink up, Frank. This here will clear your head. Yo, *Frank*!" He clapped him on the back, jolting him awake.

"Here," Leland said, skidding the cup of steaming coffee towards him.

"Oh," Frank said, staring dubiously at the coffee.

"Down the hatch with it now."

"I don't sleep good with too much coffee in me, Cap'n."

"You don't want to sleep too good. We got to turn out early tomorrow and start loading at Kelly's."

Frank first looked weary, then suddenly seemed to perk up. "Where be we bound then?"

"Up to the west'ard."

"Boston?"

"Lynn."

"Square-edged lumber?"

"Yep. No hardwood and all seasoned."

Frank looked confused for a few moments, and then he said, "You was just funnin' me about staying east of Rockland."

"Oh, I ain't decided about that yet. This freight to Kelly's was chartered last time we was here. Drink your coffee. Now, as I was saying, the worst of what happened to Dan is that he's still a mate — in his own vessel! Oh, he's *supposed* to be captain, everybody *calls* him Cap'n Dan, especially his wife does. But all you got to do is look and listen to see who's runnin' things aboard the *Sarah*. That wife of his, Hattie, she's got him so gasketed down ain't nothing could shake him loose now. He's all different from what he used to be, might as well be a dead man for all the life left in him. He don't really *have* any life of his own no more. And there ain't no sadder sight than to see what he is now, knowing what he was."

Frank had not taken more than a sip or two of the coffee, but he was somewhat more awake now, and seemed interested by what Leland had just been saying.

"This fellow," Frank said slowly and seriously, "he has his wife and his daughter *aboard* of him?"

"That's right," Leland said, warming to the response from Frank. "They go in the *Sarah* right along with him."

Frank frowned. "My father says women aboard is bad luck. He told me how he knew a ship where the captain took a woman passenger and first the ship went aground going down over the shoals, then two men went overboard and got drowned, then six more took sick and died, and finally the ship went down in a storm with all hands."

Leland's eyes about doubled in brightness. "Well, there now, you see? And you was getting sweet on one of Clara's worthless joy girls."

Frank jolted back in his chair as if Leland had slapped him in the face, or tried to.

"Susanna ain't worthless. She ain't like that. She's different." Frank seemed to search for words, but found none and just looked at Leland.

"No she ain't. You just *think* she's different. That's how it starts. First a man thinks a woman is different from other women, then he gets in over his head, and then next thing he wakes up and finds out he's married, and that's when he begins to find out slow or fast that his woman is just like all other women — worthless, foolish, underhanded, full of idiotic notions about everything, and that she intends to run his life for him and tell him what he can and can't do. Some men are a long time finding out how big a mistake they've made, and some I guess never find it out. I don't think poor Dan knows it yet, though if you see how it is with them two you find it hard to believe, her ordering him around all the time and him meekly doing everything she says. It's ruined him for a sailor."

Frank looked worried. He didn't say anything.

"Let's lower away the yawl-boat," Leland said. "We'll have a gam along o' him and you'll see it for yourself."

Frank was thoroughly awake now, full of his troubled thoughts.

They went on deck and aft to the davits, and lowered away the yawl-boat.

Once in it and with the brand-new, one-cylinder engine started, Frank said suddenly, "I asked Susanna to marry me, and she said yes, soon as I got a mate's berth and pay."

"Is that so. You'll need more'n mate's pay. By the time a woman of her type gets fairly aholt of you you'll wish you'd had a considerable longer head start to try to keep up with her money-spending notions."

———————

2

The *Sarah* was about seventy years old and she looked it. She had never been meant for speed, and age had done nothing to improve either her speed or her looks. She sat on the water with the attitude of a tired fat woman past the point of caring how she appears. Caulking sagged from gaping seams, paint was blistering, her topsides were streaked with rust from the butt spikes, chain plates, and various other ironwork. What shape she had once had, had faded into the form that relied most on the support of the water and least on her own strength. She was so badly hogged that her sheer was just about straight — except for the humps at her chain plates.

Leland steered the yawl-boat around the *Sarah* before going alongside.

"You can *smell* the rot in her," Leland said to Frank.

Frank looked the schooner over with a doubtful expression.

When they bumped alongside, Dan Procter's daughter Ann was right there to take the painter. She was seventeen years old, with clear open features and little consciousness of her own grace. Her long brown hair was all tucked out of view under a man's slouch hat, and her baggy man's shirt, work pants, and boots almost managed to make her look like a boy. In fact, most people, seeing her at any distance, did assume her to be a boy.

She glanced at Frank and nodded cordially. Then she looked at Leland and her face opened up into a dazzling smile.

"Hello, Captain Wells," she said.

" 'Lo, Ann," Leland said, somewhat stiffly, looking aft over her head.

Ann's mother, Hattie, had emerged from the after cabin and was coming towards them, her firm footfalls resounding on the deck. She was about the opposite of her daughter in all respects, being solidly and broadly built with about as much grace as a sand barge, yet wearing a dress and even earrings and perfume. She should have been a steamer captain, according to Leland's reckoning, since as far as he could see she did everything with that sort of imperious disregard for everything and everybody around her, caring nothing about who she might run down and sink.

Behind her came Dan Procter, his once-lean-and-bony form now stooped and carrying a paunch. In the old days, before he married Hattie, he would come striding along the deck with a big grin on and look glad to see you and start cracking jokes and want to know what schooners you'd been in since he saw you last, or how your schooner was doing these days. And he'd remember right off what you'd had trouble with or complained about the last time he'd seen you and want to know how you were making out now on those things, even if he hardly knew you and hadn't seen you in a couple of years. People were always amazed at Dan Procter's memory.

But now he just shuffled along, following his wife around like a mongrel pup, smiling sort of apologetically from a distance, always preoccupied and bemused.

"Well, Leland," Hattie said in her deep challenging voice. "We haven't seen you in months." As if he'd spent them in some way he'd be ashamed to admit to.

Leland looked at Dan and decided not to say the first thing that came to mind — that some people have freights to haul and not so much time for gamming as others might.

"I expect I've been so busy I ain't even noticed the time a-flying by," Leland said, doing his best to make it sound like an apology out of consideration for Dan's feelings.

"And who's this young man?" Hattie asked, turning her attention to Frank. "I don't suppose I should expect a bachelor to remember his manners enough to introduce him to us."

"That's Frank Chase," Leland said. "He started with me this spring. Frank this is Ha—"

"Hello, Frank," Hattie broke in, with, for her, an extraordinary warmth, holding out her hands to him. "I'm Hattie Procter, and this is my daughter Ann. Come here, Ann, and say hello to Frank."

Ann edged closer to Leland. Frank didn't even glance at her. He was stepping awkwardly from one foot to the other, squinting as though Hattie's eager anxiety was dazzling as the sun. He finally took Hattie's outstretched hands.

"Where are you from?" Hattie asked him. "Isn't he a handsome lad?" she asked Ann. "Don't be impolite, Ann dear. Come and greet our guest. She's so shy!"

"Larboard," Frank said, and when Hattie looked blank he added, "That's where I'm from, Larboard."

"Oh, yes," she said. "We've been there. Ann . . . "

Ann smiled apologetically at Frank. "Hello," she said. "It's very nice to meet you."

Leland had been watching Frank through all this with a sort of grim little smile. He thought he would leave it to Frank to deal with the whole business himself. Maybe that would give him some idea of what dealing with women could be like.

" 'Lo," Frank said. Hattie finally let go of his hands and he looked all around, tipping his head this way and that and weaving around the way he often did when embarrassed or trying to figure out how he ought to act. Once or twice he started to hold out his hand to Ann, but drew it back before extending it very far, since she didn't make any move to hold out hers.

"Do you like working for Captain Wells?" Ann asked him, completely self-possessed.

"Sure," Frank said, obviously grateful to have something familiar to talk about. "The *Harraseeket* is a fast schooner. And easy to handle — why you just have to turn the wheel and she goes where you point her."

"But is Captain Wells hard to work for?" she asked, with a sideways glance at Leland.

Frank looked surprised — it was quite possible he'd never thought of this question before — and he frowned at Leland.

"Naw," he said finally. "Cap'n Wells is real good. O' course, there's not as much time for taking it easy on the *Harraseeket* as they is on some. But I don't mind that. I like to work." He grinned at Leland.

Leland was thinking: He does, too, and he's a good sailor. And when he ain't up on some half-tide ledge of a girl he's pretty reliable. It would be a shame for him to get lashed down to a wife.

"Well!" Hattie said. "Ann, bring our guests aft. I'm sure they would like something to drink. Of course," she said pointedly, "when someone mentions something to drink you bachelors will be thinking of rum, but there is no alcohol aboard *this* vessel." Hattie was a great supporter of the Sturgis Bill, which had just been passed to enforce Maine's old Prohibitory Law.

Leland kept his mouth closed firmly, leaving it to Frank to think what might be said to this.

"Oh, that's all right," Frank said. "Cap'n Wells won't have any alcohol or drinkin' aboard the *Harraseeket* either, so I'm used to it."

Hattie gave Leland a dubious glance. "Of course I couldn't expect a couple of bachelors to tell a respectable married woman about their carousing and suchlike."

Frank looked baffled, opened his mouth, closed it, then opened it again. But in the end he shut it once more and said nothing.

They all trooped aft. Hattie led the way, talking all the while to Frank about the evils of drink and the virtues of being a settled, married man with responsibilities. Dan, who had stayed circumspectly on the outskirts of everything, circled out of the way of them all and brought up the rear. Leland, right behind Hattie, was grimly glad she was her usual self today and Frank was getting a good dose of her. He paid no attention to Ann, who walked silently beside him as closely as she dared, gravely erect.

As they reached the break in the deck at the forward end of the after house, Hattie broke off her one-sided conversation with Frank and threw back over her shoulder, "I'll need more water for the coffee, Cap'n Dan." Then she went right on telling Frank a little tale about a young man she once knew who wanted to marry a certain beautiful girl but who got drunk and fell off a barn roof he was shingling and was killed. Dan stopped at the starboard water barrel, and Leland turned back to take advantage of the chance to visit with him. Ann hovered a couple of steps away.

"Ann," Hattie called, pausing at the companionway. "Come get your father the bucket."

Dan nodded encouragingly at his daughter. She glanced sideways at Leland and then went up onto the quarterdeck.

"Ain't she something though?" Dan said, looking after her with a fond smile. "It's not every man fathers a daughter like that, I can tell you."

"The last time I had a gam along o' you, you were talking about trying to raise some money for repairs, maybe buy an engine for your yawl-bo't. You know I ain't much on newfangled contraptions, but I think that Knox I got in my yawl-bo't is worth the money. Saves a lot of waiting for tide and wind."

Dan's glow of pride faded into a sort of distracted annoyance. "You don't know how hard it is when you've got a family to support. It's hard to put anything by, what with freight prices as low as they is and the old *Sarah* as old as she is."

Leland was wishing Frank were hearing this.

"I've found it still helps to have a hand," Leland said. "A hand more than pays his way, if he ain't paid too overmuch."

"The old *Sarah* would never pay a hand's worth more than what she pays now. Ann's pretty good for a hand. Worth a boy at least, though not so much when it comes to loadin' and dischargin'. I used to have two hands — you remember that. But freight prices is just so low and getting lower all the time, and the hands was always paintin' the town, you know. Hattie didn't like that. So I got that donkey engine off'n that old wrack of the *George Jackson* and I dunno but what it come out cheaper in the end. With that I can sail her with just Ann's help. There's more waitin' for a good chance along than I'd like, but the *Sarah*'s gettin' pretty loose now anyway so maybe it comes out about the same in the end. I cal'late to get one of them engines for the yawl-bo't some day — Hattie's always talking about it, so I guess I'll get one sooner or later. But right now there ain't no money for that."

"You'd ought to had a son."

Dan laughed. "Well, Lee, I cal'lated to have one, but Hattie and the Good Lord cal'lated different. But I ain't complainin'. We get by one way or another, and Ann is pretty much of a help, as I said before."

The conversation went on for some minutes about this and that — freight prices, the weather, the latest race between the Tilton brothers in the *Abner S. Green* and the *Gracie Tilton*.

Then Leland said, "I guess Ann must have forgot about the bucket."

Dan scratched his head. "That ain't like her," he said. He looked puzzled a moment, and then he said, "I know what 'tis. Hattie's collared her to make a match up of her with that hand of yourn. The woman can't let her alone about that. Let a man come in hailing distance and Hattie's got him halfway to married to Ann. The woman is terrified Ann'll die an old maid, though she ain't but just seventeen. But there ain't no gettin' ahead of Hattie, you know," Dan added philosophically, as though Hattie were as inevitable and impossible to influence as the weather.

"Well then," said Leland, "there's no use our waitin' around here."

The after cabin of the *Sarah* was fairly large as such cabins went — a big selling point with Hattie, and therefore one reason Dan bought the schooner (the other reason was the low price). When Ann was about three or four years old, Hattie had prevailed on Dan to partition off the forward starboard corner, where their bedstead was. (She had insisted on the lubberly bedstead from the beginning — "I'm not sleeping in a pigeonhole," she said, referring to the existing berths built into the port and starboard bulkheads.) Dan not being much of a carpenter, this partition was somewhat crude, but it effectively closed off an area for a bedroom. Ann slept in one of the regular berths over to port. Not long after Dan built the first partition, Hattie insisted he partition off the area around Ann's berth. The hands, when they had had them, bunked forward in the forecastle, now occupied by the donkey engine.

When Dan and Leland entered the cabin they found Frank cornered against the galley counter, Hattie by the stove, and Ann standing next to her with a look of long-suffering patience. Hattie broke off whatever she had been saying; she did not seem particularly pleased that they had interrupted. Frank, sweat gleaming on his brow, looked pleadingly at Leland.

Leland opened his mouth to give Hattie the news that Frank apparently had not yet brought himself to break to her, but then he checked himself. This was supposed to be a lesson to Frank, and the boy ought to get the full effect of it. Hattie was in fine form today, and it would be a shame to disturb the natural course of events.

He satisfied himself with hefting the coffeepot that was beginning to steam and commenting, "Seems you had water enough after all," just to let her know he had been aware of her real motives all along.

"Well," Hattie said testily, "I didn't know that Ann had already gotten some. The girl never will tell a body what she's up to."

The coffee was poured after a bit, and they all sat around talking of this and that, getting around to politics and an argument about whether the surge of Progressive reform was good or bad. The argument went around and around as most such arguments do, each person sounding off about the issue of importance to him or her without much regard for what the others were saying. Though he himself was dead set against alcohol and wouldn't have so much as a bottle of patent medicine aboard, and though he had no love for the railroads and their monopolies, Leland hated any sign of the government interfering in people's lives and thought suffrage for women would only make the interference worse. As far as he was concerned, the influence of women on the country was too strong already, and what was needed was for people to be tough-minded and look after their own affairs. Hattie thought that what was needed was women voting and strict enforcement of the Prohibitory Law. She thought that most of the world's evils would be swept away by these two things. What mother in her right mind would send her son off to war? she asked. And if he could be kept safe from rum and if he was married to a good woman there would be prosperity and peace.

Dan tried to moderate and please both his wife and his guest. Frank didn't say too much, but when he did speak up he brought in a "my father always says" for authority and talked about how maybe it wasn't too good an idea to outlaw rum because a lot of people needed it for a medicinal — didn't his own mother depend on her daily dose of Peruna? — and he couldn't see what was wrong with a sailor drinking rum so long as he did it mostly while he was ashore and just waiting for another berth anyway. Ann mostly kept silent, but when she did speak it was always to defend Leland against her mother.

So a good part of the evening passed. Frank began to nod towards sleep finally, and even Leland and Hattie began to wear down. Dan was yawning, and Ann sat at the galley table with her head propped on the heel of her hand, the brim of her battered old slouch hat pulled down against the lantern light.

Eventually a silence fell, and it drew on for some moments; but then Leland thought again of Frank's news, and decided it was time to stir the fire.

"Frank," he said, "I guess you never mentioned your plans, did you?"

Frank jolted awake, sucking his breath in sharply. His eyes ran blankly over the Procters and he ended up glazedly regarding Leland. Hattie's brow furrowed.

"Frank says he's going to get married."

Hattie's mouth dropped open, then closed with a snap. She gave Leland a quick glare — which he savored to the fullest — and then she reached for the startled Frank and hugged him.

"Oh, that's *wonderful* news," she said. "And you not letting on to me! You might have told me and kept me from making a fool of myself and Ann. But that's all right, of course, you're just bashful. Who is she? Anybody we might know?"

"Her name is Susanna," Frank said modestly, but he was white in the face and quivering slightly.

"Susanna," Hattie breathed, as though the very name refreshed her. "Susanna who, dear?"

Frank gave a last pleading glance at Leland, sweat beading on his forehead now, and said, "I think her last name is Parsons."

"You *think*!" Hattie held him at arm's length and gazed into his eyes with a mixture of surprise and amusement and motherly concern.

"Well, yes. I mean, I'm pretty sure. I mean, that *is* her last name, only . . . "

"Only what, dear?" Hattie pressed him.

"Nothing." The sweat coursed down. "That's her name, only there are probably a lot of Susanna Parsons around and so it might not be the one you might think it was."

Hattie considered him narrowly, trying to figure him out. "I'm not sure I know *any* Susanna Parsons," she said. "Whereabouts might she live?"

"Up to Portland," Frank said.

"Oh, well, Portland is such a big place I don't know everybody there. I don't think I know any Parsons there. Do we, Cap'n Dan?"

Dan snapped off another yawn short and looked thoughtful, and then gravely shook his head in the negative. Leland didn't know whether Dan was still up on who the girls were at Clara Hastings' or the other establishments. He suspected not. Dan wouldn't risk Hattie's ire by even thinking about those girls. Most of them weren't even as attractive as Hattie anyway, and Hattie was at least clean.

"I don't know any Parsons anywhere west of Small Point," Hattie said. "Is she related to any Parsons here to Rockland?"

"I don't think so," Frank said. "I think all her people are there to Portland and from Scarborough." After mentioning the last place he looked as though he wished he hadn't.

Hattie looked thoughtful, but after a tense moment for Frank, she shook her head reluctantly and said, "No, I don't know any Parsons to Scarborough. Well, you must bring her to see us as soon as you can! When's the marriage to be?"

"It ain't been settled yet. I got to get at least a mate's berth first."

"Well, you just let us know if there's anything we can do."

Leland and Frank took their leave then, and all the Procters went with them to the waist of the schooner where the yawl-boat was tied alongside to starboard. It was a quiet night, the water lapping peacefully at the boats.

As Frank and Leland were about to climb over the side, Hattie said, "Now you do right by Susanna, Frank, and you'll be a happy man and settled. Not like Leland here. Don't you pay attention to him."

They climbed down, neither of them saying anything.

"Good night, Captain Wells," Ann said in a soft ringing tone into the silence.

Leland didn't look up from the engine he was about to start.

"So long, everybody," he said, and spun the flywheel. The engine coughed and began to fire and Ann cast off the painter, Frank catching and stowing it, and they turned and putt-putted across to the *Harraseeket*.

Hattie and Dan returned to the cabin as soon as their guests left, but Ann stood watching until the yawl-boat had been rigged for towing at the stern of the *Harraseeket*, and Leland had followed Frank below.

3

Leland and Frank and the stevedores at the lumber dock were still finishing up the deckload on the *Harraseeket* when the *Sarah*, along with a few other schooners, drifted east beyond the Rockland

Breakwater. In the *Sarah*'s hold was a small shipment of lumber and on deck a load of screwed hay covered with canvas. Since there had been no sign of mist over the Camden Hills the day before, the expectation of all was that today fog was unlikely. It was a warm morning, the sun shining clear and bright with the wind beginning to make up out of the south, blowing north the haze from the lime kilns. The tide had just peaked around ten thirty.

Aboard the *Harraseeket*, Leland was hurrying things along all he could, anxious to clear port, cussing Frank and the stevedores, the latter cussing him back. Overhead, the scandalized main and foresail, left up to dry, flapped idly, the booms hoisted up so as to be out of the way of the mounting deckload of hemlock, spruce, and fir.

Leland kept looking out beyond the breakwater at the sails of the schooners that had managed to get away with the first of the wind, especially at the *Sarah*. Something irritated him about leaving port behind that boat, never mind that she should have left days ago, having arrived here ahead of him with nothing more to do but put aboard a deckload of hay.

The southerly didn't hold for long. When it fushed out altogether, the schooners were in a scatter out near Owls Head. Their sails hung limp and their bows swung this way and that depending on how they rode the long deep easterly swell rolling in from some storm that had passed by at sea.

At the dock it was hot. Smoke from the lime kilns greyed the sky. The men sweated and their cursing carried all along the waterfront. Then the stevedores stopped for lunch. Leland made some choice comments about union labor and jumped onto the dock and began passing the boards to Frank. Frank sweated a continuous river, but Leland never gave him break enough to have so much as a sip of water.

The stevedores were not in any particular hurry coming back from lunch; by the time they reappeared Leland and Frank were on the last few layers. As soon as the stevedores took up the work of passing the boards over the rail, Leland set Frank to making sure all the lines led fair and tying in lumber reefs in the fore and main — the reefs had been shaken out after unloading at the Maine Central wharf.

By this time the wind had begun to breathe lightly out of the northeast and the schooners that had been drifting aimlessly began to lay courses for Owls Head Bay, Two Bush Channel, or Fox Islands Thorofare, or began beating up the bay. The *Sarah*, for all her age and sagging hull, seemed to scud with merry, youthful flirtatiousness before the quickly freshening breeze into Owls Head Bay.

"She's out," Frank said, referring to the easterliness of the wind, which meant fog could roll in. Leland shrugged.

Aloft aboard the *Harraseeket* sails began to flap. Leland drove Frank and himself with renewed energy. Yet it was nearly two o'clock before they managed to clear away, what with one thing and another. Leland was in a foul mood by this time, and Frank knew enough of Leland's temper to stay away from him and try to do everything he was told immediately and perfectly. But it was impossible not to cross him one way or another. If Frank waited until given the order to do something that was obviously going to need doing, Leland demanded why he was so slow to act. "Never get a mate's berth you don't smarten up, boy," Leland told him with a kind of grim relish. But if Frank tried to anticipate an order and do something before he was asked to, Leland was likely to glare at him and demand, "Just who do you figure's master of this schooner?" When Frank would mumble something like, "Well, you are, Cap'n," Leland would bellow, "Don't talk back to me, son. Just follow orders is all I ask. It ain't much, even for you."

But once they cleared the breakwater and were fairly boiling along close-hauled for Owls Head with the whole of Penobscot Bay blue and dazzlingly bright in the sun around them — no sign of fog yet — Leland turned over the helm to Frank and went below and came up shortly with an apple pie he'd found time to make amidst all the work of loading. He served Frank up about a third of it, cut another third for himself, and then took the helm to give Frank a chance to concentrate on the pie. When Frank had cleaned up his portion, he cast furtive glances at the remaining third, not saying anything. Leland, almost finished his own share, allowed as how he'd had enough pie for now and Frank could eat the rest if he had a mind to. "No use to let it set," he said. "Pies don't improve with age."

A minute or two later, as he was scraping up the last of it from his plate, Frank said, "That's awful good pie, Cap'n."

"I reckon a pie is a pie," Leland said.

"Well, maybe. But I'd rather have it than one of my own mother's, and she makes real good pies."

"Oh, women don't really know that much about cooking. They just do it because they're good for nothing else, but they don't have no scientificness about it."

"Well, maybe that's why *I* can't never cook anything, or my father either. Course, he never figured it was man's work anyway. But I guess I just ain't smart enough to do it the way a man ought to, and I ain't no woman and so can't do it by guess and by gorry — a pinch of this and a dash of that, the way my mother does." Frank's face clouded up as he pondered all this. After a bit he said, "I know I ain't really all that smart. Tell me honest now, do you think I'll ever get a mate's berth?"

Leland frowned. Once one of his tempers had subsided and he had done something to amend for it, he disliked to be reminded of the unkind things he'd said.

"Oh, of course you'll get a mate's berth," he said testily. "And you'll get married and hauled up ashore to rot just like your father. If you *were* smart, you'd either find a good lee and anchor, or else haul onto the wind and beat to sea before the weather closes in. But you won't, any more than most men. I got no more to say about it." He picked up the empty plates and forks and stalked for the companionway. There, he turned back for a moment and said, "Ain't day enough left to bother going out to Two Bush. We'll go through the bay and into the Mussel Ridges." Then he went below.

They had turned the corner and scudded the length of Owls Head Bay and were headed into the Mussel Ridge Channel by the time the next change in the day came. The wind slacked off, grew fitful, and finally fushed out. By that time a heavy silvery-topped bank of fog had hove in sight offshore, pushing in towards them.

"Well, ain't this just the damnedest day for weather," Frank said, and spat over the rail. He stood proud-chested, hands on his hips, legs braced a bit apart on the deck, looking straight out to sea.

They lay becalmed inside the inner Grindstone Ledges, the broken swell slamming gear with a dismal sound. The blue sky overhead had lost its clarity and was greying, the sun growing slightly fuzzy. Then came the measured double bong of the fog signal away off on Two Bush, and shortly after the steam whistle on Whitehead joined it. There was a sudden change in the feel of the air, an ominous chill.

The *Harraseeket* had a good compass and Leland took care to check it for accuracy every chance he got. Yet the compass was not included in his automatic glance around to get his bearings. It never was. The compass was used only for giving Frank something to steer by. Among Maine skippers, none of whom could amount to a capful

– 83 –

of wind without some ability to navigate in the fog, Leland Wells was considered to have nearly supernatural powers.

Fog on the Maine coast can close in with frightening speed, and so it was in this case. The wall of grey rolled over them in jig time, and in a matter of minutes there was nothing to see but the schooner, and not all of that clearly, the tip of the jibboom hovering on the far edge of visibility. Sometimes fog will close in thickly outside while the Mussel Ridge Channel remains fairly clear, but not this time. The light southeasterly breeze brought the fog across the deck in eerie almost-forms like big amorphous ghosts that might or might not actually be there. The booms slammed over with a dull thudding and their clattering muffled, and the schooner began to move again. They hauled onto the wind. Behind them the Owls Head bell started up.

"If this ain't a thick-o-fog," Frank said.

"Well, it might be a mite thick now, at that," Leland said. "You can let her off a spoke, if you want to . . . that's about it. What d'she say now?"

"Right about dead sou'west, Cap'n."

"Well then, just hold to that for a spell."

They eased along on the damp breeze for some minutes, seeing nothing. The rollers became a smaller, more confused sea. There might have been the sound of the new bell buoy at Otter Island that the steamship line had paid for.

"Now you can let her off a mite more," Leland said.

"We're inside the Mussel Ridges for fair now," Frank said a little later. "That swell is all broke up."

On they glided, seeing nothing but fog, yet Leland seemed to have no doubts. Now and then he altered course a bit for no reason that would have been apparent to anyone who didn't know the channel. Several times they might have heard surf — or might not have — and there were the fog signals, yet sounds are peculiar in the fog, and distance and direction figured from sounds none too reliable. They never saw Otter Island Ledge, Garden Island Ledge, Hurricane Ledge, or Yellow Ridge Island, nor did they see any of the eight buoys and spindles along the channel marking these and other hazards. They sailed nearly six miles without Leland checking the time, looking for a buoy, consulting a chart, or even glancing at the compass.

The whistle at Whitehead had been seeming fairly close for some little while and the big easterly swell was back when they heard surf to leeward and felt the jostling of the backwash from the cliffs of Whitehead. Suddenly they heard a bell buoy off to port and Leland said, "That'll be South Breaker. Ease her up into the wind a mite." He tended sheets, bringing the booms inside the rail. The *Harraseeket* creaked and heeled a little more. Leland came aft again. "What d'she say now?"

" 'Bout sou'west by south."

"Well then, keep her so."

They sailed on, making about five or six knots, the breeze having picked up out in the open, perhaps having gained something from the tide now on the make. The fog was a bit thicker out here and Frank felt justified referring to it as a thick dungeon of fog, though Leland never referred to it as more than a mite thick. From the helm you could just see the mainmast.

It was getting on for six o'clock, a couple of hours having passed since leaving what Leland had identified as South Breaker — two eerie hours disturbed only by the passing of two steamboats, which brought on an extra tension of watchfulness and some muttered curses from Leland — when the sound of surf seemed to come suddenly from right under their bowsprit.

"You don't have to sail her right over the Roaring Bull," Leland said. "All we wanted was to find it."

Frank swung the wheel over and they dropped to leeward.

"I smell hay," Frank said suddenly.

The smell was strong enough not to be mistaken.

"Ain't no hayfields out here," Frank said in a serious voice.

"Somebody's to windward with a deckload of hay," Leland said with an air of bringing the subject to a close.

"Maybe it's the *Sarah* then," Frank said. "They was headed this way. Whoever 'tis they must be pretty close to the Roaring Bull."

After a moment more Frank said, "Wait, listen. Ain't that somebody hollering?"

Leland glared into the fog. As he made out Ann's voice emerging from the roar of the breakers like the thin cry of a seabird, there came back to him a dream he'd had the previous night about heaving his anchor short and finding Hattie hanging on to it. Leland was not superstitious, as seamen go, but right now he had the feeling that if he responded to that cry his life would never be the same again.

Frank had never seen such a black look on the captain's face, and he shivered involuntarily.

Leland took the helm and sent Frank forward to handle the headsails. They boxhauled, using a tail rope to hold the jib aback and a watch tackle to hold the main to windward, and the *Harrasee-ket* spun around onto the other tack with dispatch. They sailed around to the north of the rock where the water was shallower than elsewhere and dropped the hook in seven fathoms onto rocky bottom. The anchor dragged, caught momentarily, dragged some more, then fetched up solid. They let out all the chain there was. Neither of them said anything about the risk of the anchor breaking loose again. They lowered away the yawl-boat and putt-putted cautiously up the lee of the Roaring Bull. As they drew close, the water became turbulent and treacherous. Still, Leland made holding his course look easy, standing at the tiller grim-visaged while the boat bobbed and shied under him. Frank, as directed, sat forward with a long-handled boathook in hand. They also had a small grapnel and some line light enough to heave.

First there was a looming something, indistinct. Then there was the *Sarah*, over on her beam ends so they were looking at her deck, which was now mostly empty of the load of screwed hay, the rotten canvas covers torn loose. She lay with her bottom to the breakers, which thundered under her, the spray rising over her. She appeared stove in on her starboard side, which was rolled down. She might well be in imminent peril of breaking up; she was old and full of rot and her shape hinted that the keel might be broken. The big rollers came in round-topped and green-grey and broke under and around the poor old schooner, and the water swirled around both her ends and rose in a heap as it met in her lee.

Ann stood on the side of the after house, waving both arms and shouting something they couldn't make out.

Leland brought the boat right up under the looming *Sarah*'s lee, the heaping seas heaving the yawl-boat up and trying to spin her around, then dropping out from under with sickening speed; but Leland kept her headed where he wanted her to head. The *Sarah*'s mainmast lay out over a patch of water that didn't show bare ledge with every retreat of the swell, and Leland put the yawl-boat there with deceptive ease. Frank, who had already had plenty of opportunity to be impressed with Leland's seamanship, kept looking around and up into the grim face of the *Harraseeket*'s master with openmouthed awe.

"Just snag that halyard there, Frank," Leland said in a flat foghorn tone.

Frank reached out and on the third try managed to get the hook on a bight of halyard that looped down. He pulled up to it.

"Make fast with the painter, but not too short now," said Leland.

Frank, who nearly got pulled out of the boat when she dropped down, had a job getting tied on, but he managed it eventually.

The peculiar thing about the *Sarah* was that the mainsail was furled and the jibs gasketed on the bowsprit, while the foresail was halfway down, slack on the peak halyard as though scandalized. The foresail bagged down in the water, the gaff dangling to just within reach of the seas when they piled up in the lee of the schooner. The tiller was broken off the rudder post. Neither Hattie nor Dan was anywhere to be seen. Leland thought maybe the tiller had broken first, then the foresail jammed when they tried to get the sails down, and something happened to Dan when he tried to clear it.

Ann had by now climbed out the ratlines to the main crosstrees, just about over the yawl-boat. Dan's words, "It's not every man fathers a daughter like that," came unbidden through Leland's mind as he looked at her up there. That was not a safe place to be with the *Sarah* jolting with every wave and threatening to break up at any moment.

"Father's hurt real bad," she shouted down to them. "Mother's below with him, but there's water in the cabin and I don't think the *Sarah*'s going to last much longer."

"Can your father walk?" Leland asked her.

"He's not even conscious. He fell and hit his head and there's blood coming out his mouth."

"You mind this boat," Leland said to Frank. "Holler if something goes wrong."

"Aye, Cap'n." Frank took an involuntary look back towards the *Harraseeket*. All there was to see was fog. If the *Harraseeket* dragged her anchor, they would never know it until they tried to find her.

Leland grabbed the slack halyard and swung up; in a moment he was following Ann along to the deck of the *Sarah*.

The after cabin was a shambles. Seawater surging from the hold had knocked out the hatch in the cabin sole, and the low side of the cabin was three or four feet deep in water, with the hatch cover floating in it amongst other debris. On the far side the door to Ann's little portside cabin hung open, and in there Dan was stretched in the trench made by the deck and the partition, with Hattie bent over him.

"Mother?" Ann called to her.

Hattie looked around.

"Leland!" she exclaimed. "Thank God, we're rescued!"

"Father went up to clear the fore throat halyard," Ann was explaining to Leland. "The tiller broke off and we were trying to get the sails down until we could fix it. But something happened and he fell. Mother and I carried him below to bed and then we struck and we lost the yawl-boat. The *Sarah* started to go over on her beam ends, and so we put Father in here. That was before the list got so bad. How can we get him out?"

Leland looked at Ann, struck by her calm and clearheadedness. Then he saw she was trembling and that her knuckles were white where she held onto the companionway slide.

"You wait a minute," Leland said, and he went forward to the main hatch. With some effort, he managed to get the hatch cover off — it slid down and floated away. He went into the hold.

In the surging water, he found a stout plank from the freight of lumber, and with this he returned to the companionway. He braced himself in it and shot the plank across to the open doorway of Ann's little compartment. With a couple of nails and a hammer Ann brought him, he managed to fix the plank so it was reasonably level athwartship, and then he and Ann crossed it.

Dan's eyes were open, and he seemed drowsily awake, gazing up at Leland with a distant, thoughtful air.

"Leland is here," Hattie said to him. "It'll be all right now."

There was a gurgly sound to Dan's breathing, and there were flecks of blood around his mouth. Hattie had cleaned off quite a bit of blood apparently — she had a bloodstained towel and a bowl of water beside her.

Dan began to speak. "I'm glad you're here," he said in a low, slurred voice. His eyes watered from the effort; Hattie dabbed them dry with the corner of her handkerchief.

"We've got to—" Leland began, but Dan started to speak again as though he hadn't heard him.

"Get out of here . . . Hattie . . . you too, Ann . . . go on . . . want to talk . . . to Lee . . . "

"I most certainly will not," Hattie said.

Dan closed his eyes as though against a stab of pain. "Please . . ." he said. "Just for a minute . . . I promise not to die . . . while you're away . . ." The expression on his face didn't change, so it wasn't clear if he intended a joke.

Hattie glanced up at Leland, and he was startled to see her looking frightened and uncertain.

Leland nodded at her, and she got reluctantly to her feet and cautiously crossed the wide plank to the companionway. Ann followed.

Then Leland squatted next to Dan.

"The Old Man . . . is calling me aft," Dan said in a weary tone. "I can't move anything . . . feel anything . . . Lee . . . "

"I'm here," Leland said, and leaned further over to make it easier for Dan to see him.

Dan studied him with eyes that seemed not to focus well, and then there came over his face a hint of an ironic smile, though filled with a kind of sympathy. He gazed at Leland with an unnatural steadiness.

"Lee . . . I want you to . . . promise me . . . there's nobody, you know. . . Hattie's got no people . . . I don't . . . there's nobody . . . and now the *Sarah*'s gone . . ." He closed his eyes, the eyelids looking old and leathery and almost reptilian. Then he opened his eyes again and seemed to have difficulty focusing on Leland's face. "You're the best man I know. . . I'd never trust anybody else . . . please . . ."

Leland felt the anger bulging in him. Yet he'd known this was coming. There was no way out. He couldn't blame Dan, except for being fool enough to get married in the first place.

"I'll see to them while they need it," Leland said in a terse voice.

Dan's eyes closed for a moment, and then he looked again at Leland.

"Thanks . . ." he whispered. "Ann . . . she . . . you'll see . . ."

4

They got off the schooner as soon as they could. Hattie turned out to be more trouble than Dan's body. She was not only without agility, but was terrified of all types of climbing. She had been brought up in a town, a baker's daughter, and eighteen years a schoonerman's wife, spent entirely aboard his vessel, had changed her attitudes and outlook very little.

For quite a while she would not even discuss the question of how she should be conveyed from the deck to the yawl-boat. She seemed interested only in taking off all manner of possessions, directing this operation in a booming voice and with much gesticulation.

Ann, pale and with chilled, shaking hands, hurried to do her mother's bidding, patient when her own suggestions were cut short only to be thrown back at her a moment later by a Hattie irritated that Ann hadn't thought of these things herself. Both women might have been near tears some of the time, but neither wept, as Leland was in a sweat they would.

Leland slung a bosun's chair on a block and tackle beneath a mainmast hoop, cut the hoop loose of the mainsail, slushed the mast, and put a line on the rig so as to haul it out over the yawl-boat. The hard thing was to get Hattie into the chair. She was by turns hysterically demanding and obstinately uncooperative.

By the time she was ensconced in the yawl-boat, she was ashen and exhausted, yet she was no sooner settled and Frank about to cast off than she said, "Mother's teapot! Ann dear, did you bring it?"

"No," said Ann.

"Oh, how could you leave it! I *must* have Mother's teapot."

"We've been long enough as it is," Leland said. "Forget the teapot. You can get another one."

"Not *this* one," Hattie said. "This was my mother's. My father sent it to her from down south during the Rebellion and it was the last thing he sent before he was killed. Of course I can't leave it behind."

"We're lucky to get away from here without being put to more trouble than we have been already," Leland said.

"I'll go," Ann said kindly to her mother, and stood up.

"You will not," Leland said. When Ann gave him a look of surprise and hurt, he added irritably, "I'm not having you taking any more chances around that old wreck. I'll go, if anybody does."

"Oh, thank you, Leland," Hattie said with a rush of feeling and gratitude. "It would mean so much to me. Do you know where to look?"

"I didn't say I *would* go," he began, but the discomfiting sense that both women were about to cry made him mutter, "Oh the hell with it," under his breath, and then, louder, "I'll go, but next time don't be so quick to figure I've said something I haven't."

So it was that he went back for a teapot. Then they cast off and a moment later were in the fog with nothing in sight. Leland took a heading with as much assurance as if he could see the *Harraseeket* at anchor, and a couple of minutes later she hove out of the fog right over the bow of the yawl-boat. For some minutes they were occupied getting themselves, Dan's body, and the salvage aboard the *Harraseeket*.

"I can put you ashore at Port Clyde," Leland said. "You ought to be able to get the *Sarah* hauled off tomorrow, if she's still there. I don't know if it'll be worth it or not. There may be somebody going light who'd be interested in trying to get that lumber wherever 'twas you was going. But if you ask me she won't last the night and that lumber will be all over the place."

"Oh, I don't know what to do," Hattie said, sounding distressed. "I guess it doesn't matter much anymore. None of Dan's people are alive now. Of course, they was all down to Eastport."

"I can't go all the way down to Eastport now," Leland said. "I've got to get this lumber up to Lynn. You could get there on a packet probably. Or maybe somebody going that way might take you down."

"It's so awful! My poor Dan! And everything gone. Whatever are we going to do?"

Leland pressed his lips hard together for a moment, and then he said, "I guess you'll find something all right. Can you sew good? Maybe you could do that."

"It'll be so lonely at the funeral, just Ann and I. Dan knew quite a lot of people, but I don't know who might bother to go to his funeral. *You'll* be there, won't you?" she said, looking earnestly at Leland, then at Frank, who hadn't said a word since seeing Dan's body carried out of the *Sarah*'s after cabin wrapped in sheets.

When Leland said nothing, Frank finally spoke up. "Sure," he said.

"Listen," said Leland, "we've got to get off this ground. Do you want to go into Port Clyde, or some'er's else? I'm bound up to the west'ard, so anywhere else'll be further from Eastport, and from Rockland too, if you want to get a towboat up here to try hauling the *Sarah* off."

"I don't know where we'll stay," Hattie said uncertainly. "Do you know anybody there?"

"Well, there must be some kind of charity there or somewheres not too far off for widows and orphans," Leland said, reasonably.

Hattie looked devastated. She put her face in her hands and began to sob. Ann comforted her.

"*Now* what's the matter?" Leland demanded querulously. He was beginning to have a hunted look.

Because of the fog and approaching darkness, the *Harraseeket*'s after cabin was very dim. Frank suddenly set about lighting the oil lamp mounted on the bulkhead over the table at which Ann and her mother were sitting. When the lamp began to brighten the gloom a little, Hattie looked up at it, her eyes red and her cheeks wet.

"All I meant to say," said Leland, "was that just because you don't know anybody there doesn't mean there might not be somebody happy to give you a place to stay for a few days until you get a chance to make your own arrangements. If you don't have enough money . . ."

"Oh, I've got *money*," Hattie said with disgust. "Anyway, I wouldn't hear of taking any of *yours*. You just put us ashore, and we'll find some way to get along." She lifted her chin, setting it.

Leland frowned, but all he said was, "All right then, come on, Frank, let's heave short."

Leland took the *Harraseeket* into Port Clyde on the dying southeasterly and anchored off the wharves. They put Dan's body and all the things Hattie and Ann had taken off the *Sarah* into the yawlboat. Everything, that is, except the teapot.

"I don't want it to get broken," Hattie explained. "If I am to be moving around, there's no telling what might happen to it. But if it is left packed away in that cupboard in your galley, it'll be safe. You don't really mind, do you? You'll be sure nothing happens to it? And when I'm settled somewhere, I'll come and get it. It'll be such a comfort to know it is somewhere safe! You have no idea what your taking the trouble to go back and get that teapot means to me, Leland. That's all I have now of my own family."

"I don't really see why your teapot wouldn't be safer with you than with me," Leland said. "You ought to know how things are in a vessel. There might be some weather or something . . ."

"But you see, I've wrapped it all up and packed it in this little box Frank found for me. If you just keep it there in the cupboard, it'll be perfectly safe. And you'd be doing me such a favor, Leland, taking such a load of care off my shoulders. Wouldn't you do that for me?"

Leland had an idea that there was more to Hattie's reasoning than met the eye, but for the moment he was stuck with the teapot, and as he saw it that was better than being stuck with Hattie and Ann.

At the same time he was thinking this, he was also remembering Joe Parker, who sometimes wanted a load of lumber hauled to Portland or some such place. Joe or his wife might know where Hattie and Ann could stay — Leland decided he would take the women to the Parkers' house and see what might be found out.

Sally Parker opened the door to them, and the conversation had lasted only a few moments before she realized what the situation was and began insisting they stay there with her.

"The children are all grown," she said. "There's plenty of room for you right here. I'll send Joe to get the undertaker."

She also insisted that Leland and Frank stay to supper and tell the whole story, which she kept interrupting with a lot of oohing and aahing and praise of everybody — Leland and Frank for their heroic rescue of the women, and Ann and Hattie for their fortitude and good luck in being rescued. And then she told them about how things had been when her first husband was killed trying to dismantle a barn; how horrible the death was and how she kept dreaming about it and waking up at night shaking, how she had thought the world had ended for her, but how in time it had all passed and she had married Joe and they had raised a wonderful big family, and how blessed her life seemed now and how proud of all her children she was. She went on to tell about them and their doings, and she told how happy they all were and went on in this fashion for some time, her bright perceptive eyes all the while gauging the effect of her efforts on Hattie and Ann. Then, suddenly, her chatter veered: "And you must be very proud of your beautiful daughter here!" she exclaimed to Hattie. "I have two wonderful daughters, but neither one is as beautiful as Ann is! I guess a mother shouldn't say something like that, should she!" She smiled impishly at Ann, who sat very straight in her chair, with her eyes cast down, blushing.

"I'll bet Frank here has noticed she's pretty," she added slyly.

Now Frank was blushing, though he also looked preoccupied.

But when Ann glanced up, it wasn't at Frank, it was at Leland. He and Joe sat back from the table, just barely within the circle of lantern light, ankles on knees, Joe smoking his pipe. They had been talking in low tones about the best thing to do about the *Sarah*, and Leland had gotten Joe to say he would look after the thing as best he could for the benefit of the women. They had fallen silent just before Sally made her sly comment, but when Ann glanced up at Leland he didn't let on.

Sally Parker's eyes followed Ann's glance to Leland and played there speculatively for a moment.

"Well!" she said, pressing her palms together. "Here I've been jabbering on, and I expect you're all tired and want some rest."

Leland stood up.

"I'd ought to be getting back to the *Harraseeket*," he said. Since setting foot ashore, he had not really looked anyone in the eye, except Joe once or twice during their conversation about the *Sarah*. He didn't look at anyone now, frowning down at the back of an empty chair.

"You'll do no such thing!" Sally exclaimed, as though affronted. "There's plenty of room here."

"That's as may be," Leland said, looking not at her but at the pattern in the linen tablecloth. "I think I ought to get back. I dislike to leave her long, loaded and all, you know."

"Why, don't you think our little harbor is safe?" Sally said, halfway mocking him, but there was an edge of urgency to her tone.

"Oh, I reckon it's safe enough," Leland said. "Comin', Frank?"

"Why, Mr. Wells," Sally said, clearly upset now, "a body would think you care more about that schooner than you do about your friends."

Leland was gazing vaguely off across the room at the clock ticking away on the mantle. One would not have believed this was the same man who was so formidable afloat.

"We got to go," he said, his eyes furtive, finding nothing easy to rest on.

They happened to meet Ann's eyes. Sally's consternation, Hattie's ashen look of unhappiness, Frank's embarrassed confusion, and even quiet Joe's slight frown of disapproval and doubt Leland could feel like a wall between him and them. But when he looked straight into Ann's warm, sympathetic eyes, his weathered face paled and he glanced quickly down, and then around desperately for the door, through which he beat a hasty retreat.

"When are you coming back?" Hattie called after him fearfully to no answer.

Frank, with practically incoherent apologies and explanations, followed a few moments later, and had to run to catch up with Leland, who strode along as though in a rage.

Once aboard the schooner, Leland's whole aspect changed. His back straightened and his eyes focused into their characteristic piercing gaze.

"Rig the yawl-boat for towing, Frank," he said briskly, and strode purposefully forward to the windlass, yanking a windlass brake from the rack with a decisive motion.

Frank was too terrified of Leland's mood to say a single word. While Leland hove short the anchor, Frank rigged the yawl-boat astern so it would behave like a little tugboat pushing the schooner from behind. He started the engine, Leland broke out the anchor, and they were gone into the foggy night.

5

They had contrary winds for nearly a week, but the *Harraseeket* was better than most schooners of her type to windward, and day after day, and even some nights when the wind held, Leland relentlessly beat her up towards Lynn. Frank staggered around the deck so tired that when he did have a chance to sleep he couldn't seem to do so. The days and nights all ran together and he had trouble remembering from one minute to the next what he had just been doing. Leland said hardly a word. He slept almost not at all, pacing the deck during the nights they were in port at anchor. Frank would lie awake in the dark, staring blankly with red eyes at the underside of the deck, listening to Leland's footfalls resounding on the other side of it. Every so often, Frank would murmur something like, "He has to wear out sometime . . . or maybe he don't . . ."

Then the wind quit and there was a fog mull that lasted for a relatively brief time as such mulls go — only a day and a half — and finally Frank slept. When he awoke, he lay looking at the sun streaming in through one of the rectangular ports onto the cabin sole. There was no sound of pacing. Frank glanced over at Leland's bunk, and there the man lay sprawled, asleep.

There was a dry northeaster. They were rolling along easily towards Lynn now, Frank slouching with careless ease at the helm, and Leland sitting up on the deckload letting his legs swing to the roll of his vessel. He was at home, his eyes keeping track of all around him, his whole being tuned to the resounding joy that the *Harraseeket* so obviously felt dancing over the bright rolling water.

For days, Frank had been turning over what he was about to say to Leland. It was his conscience that brought him to it, finally overcoming his terror of Leland's probable reaction.

"We goin' back?" he asked.

Leland looked around. "Goin' back where?"

"You know. To Port Clyde."

"And why in hell should we be fool enough to go back there?"

Frank opened his mouth and stared at Leland, trying to think what he might say to that.

"Sally and Joe will take good care of them," Leland went on when Frank said nothing. "They'll get along all right."

Leland gazed off at the horizon for a while, lost in thought. Frank still said nothing.

"Listen," Leland said, turning on him, "what business is it of mine what happens to useless women? What would *I* do with them? I don't know nothing about keeping women. Just enough to know I don't want none around me. Just what the hell would I *do* with them damn women?" He glared challengingly at Frank.

"But," Frank said before he thought, "I think Ann loves you."

"*Loves* me!" Leland gaped at Frank. "Well ain't *that* a buffle-brained notion." He was silent a moment, trying to take the thing in. "Why, I'm old enough to be her father. Anyway, it don't make a difference to me what witless notions might be in some silly girl's head."

"Well then, what you gonna do with Hattie's teapot?"

"Throw the damn thing overboard, is what *I'll* do with it." Leland glared out over the glinting water as though he could already see the teapot on its way overside.

For the next several days as they unloaded at Lynn, Frank sweated over the question of whether he ought to hide the teapot and try to get it back to Hattie on the sly. In the end he was too uncertain about his plans, and he did nothing. But Leland never went near the cupboard where the teapot resided, and so it stayed safely where it was.

After unloading, they went to Cambridgeport to load a cargo of miscellaneous appointments for a new summer house being built at Camden by a rich businessman from New York. The stuff had to be kept dry, and some of the furniture was fairly fancy, so loading it was fussy, irritating work. Before they were ready to put to sea, Leland had cussed every ancestor the rich businessman had, in addition to the man himself and each piece of furniture and everything and everybody that hove in sight while they were loading.

Then came days of beautiful dry northeasters, a rare treat for coastermen looking for a good chance along to the westward — but the *Harraseeket* was headed down east. Leland grimly beat into it, soaking the empty deck which he had not found a cargo to occupy. Every morning he'd stick his head out of the hatch and then come back in muttering, "Dry no'theaster again," and fall nearly silent the rest of the day. Frank didn't dare speak a word.

After nearly a week of this they finally got a very light and fitful southerly and drifted slowly down east under a warm and hazy sun. On that day, Leland suddenly opened up on Frank thus: "Would *you* go back there?"

Frank, who had been in a reverie composed partly of the wonder of sailing the *Harraseeket* and partly of images of Susanna, started. "Where?" he asked.

"Port Clyde — where the hell else?" Leland's jaw jutted belligerently.

"Sure," Frank said. When Leland said nothing, just glared seaward, Frank said, "They're just women. They don't have nothing much. And I'd figure I owed Dan something, maybe."

"So what am I supposed to do, look after them the rest of their lives? Women is such *useless* critters."

"Well, I dunno."

The next day they still had a fair wind, and along towards the end of the day, as they were finally sailing into Camden Harbor, Leland, who had been unusually silent and thoughtful, approached Frank at the wheel.

"I guess you know I was with Dan when he died," he said to Frank, eyeing him appraisingly as he spoke.

"Sure."

"Well," Leland said, and paused, scratching his chin. "He was worried about them — what would happen, you know."

"To Hattie and Ann?"

Leland gave Frank a sharp look, as if his trust in him had been shaken.

"Never mind," he said, and walked away.

A few days later, after unloading and setting out for Rockland to load birch flooring for Lynn, Leland said, "I guess them women don't really have nobody but us." He scrutinized Frank's face with care.

"Well, there's the Parkers."

"That's so," Leland said hopefully. "They don't seem to mind having them stay there. Hattie must be able to do *something*."

"And Ann might get married."

Leland stiffened, then relaxed. "You know, that's so, ain't it. And she'll have a damn sight better chance of snagging some fellow there ashore in the town than she would out here on the *Harraseeket*. I guess then Hattie could stay with them, couldn't she?" He glared at Frank as though challenging him to dare contradict that idea if he thought he had the nerve.

"She might," Frank said. There was just the merest hesitance of doubt in his reply.

"Well," Leland said, "he couldn't very well leave her out to starve, now could he? The girl wouldn't stand for it, and *Hattie* wouldn't. *She'd* see he didn't turn her out, I reckon."

"I reckon," Frank said, now frowning doubtfully.

Neither spoke for some little while. The light westerly they had been coaxing some headway out of had quit entirely, and they drifted, slowly turning. There was no sea running to speak of, and the water had a lazy, liquid, idle ruffle to it.

"What's Susanna's mother like?" Leland asked carefully.

"She's dead."

"Oh."

"Father's dead, too. He was a drunk, she says."

"Supposing Hattie was Susanna's mother?"

Frank scrunched up his face for a moment. "I'm glad she ain't. I don't mean nothing by it — Hattie's all right. But . . . ."

"Still, Ann ain't so bad," Leland said cautiously.

Frank looked at Leland with his eyebrows raised and his mouth slightly open. Leland lifted his chin and regarded Frank with a kind of defiant belligerence.

"What I mean to say is," he went on, "that some fellow might want her enough to take Hattie into the bargain."

"He might," Frank said noncommittally, and there the matter rested until they made Port Clyde.

6

They had been gone for over a month. Spring had really come to Maine now. There were early flowers in the gardens, green grass was everywhere, and trees were well along in leafing out. Bright mornings were full of singing birds.

The Parkers' house had a little garden with a white picket fence around it, one opening in which was arched over with Concord grape vines on a trellis. Sally Parker liked her flowers, and when Leland and Frank came through the grape arbor she was on her knees in the middle of her garden humming happily.

"Hello," Leland said.

She started around and then got hurriedly to her feet. "Leland!" she exclaimed, dropping the trowel she had been working with. She ran to them with arms outstretched, beaming all over. "How lovely to see you!" she said. "And what's this you've brought?"

"Hattie's teapot," Leland said, avoiding her gaze.

Sally took Leland's face in her earth-covered hands, pulled it towards her, and kissed him on the cheek, then did the same to Frank. Leland frowned; Frank grinned foolishly.

"Hattie and Ann are at church," she said. "But they'll be back any time now. I usually go, but it was such a nice morning . . ." She reddened.

"Well, there ain't no need of us waiting for them," Leland said. "Hattie's teapot will be safe enough with you until she gets back."

He held it out to her, but she didn't take it. She was looking down the street thoughtfully.

"The funeral was very nice," she said, "but there weren't many people there. Hattie really missed you. The *Sarah* broke up the night you left and so she got nothing out of that, poor woman."

"Where shall I put this then?" Leland said, his tone hopeless and resigned.

"Oh, I don't know. Hattie'll know what to do with it, I guess. You'll have to ask her."

Leland sighed.

"You know," Sally said, "it's funny about Ann. She absolutely will not wear a dress. She goes off to church looking like a sailor. It mortifies Hattie. Hattie says she has made her dresses, but the girl won't have anything to do with them." Sally looked up at Leland. "Why is that, do you think? And such a pretty girl, too."

"I don't know nothing about it," Leland said. "Suppose I just leave this teapot on the front steps."

"Oh no, not there! Joe is apt to come stumbling out not watching where he's going and break it. He is the worst one for not watching where he's going, I tell you. I never seen such a man as him for that. You just hang onto it. They won't be long now, and you can ask Hattie herself about it." She paused and absently dusted the drying earth off her hands, looking down the street again. "I just can't understand the girl. I wonder if she's been at sea too long. A girl like that doesn't belong off living like a sailor. And I've told her so. I tried to tell her what a sensation she would make if she put on a dress when she went to church — she really is a very pretty girl, you know — or hadn't you noticed? But oh, that *awful* hat she wears! You know what she said? She said she wishes she were a man because then maybe you would hire her on as a hand and she could support herself and her mother!"

"She said that?" Leland looked thoughtful. "She's got an uncommon level head for a girl."

"Oh good heavens," Sally said, shaking her head and throwing up her hands. She turned back to her garden for a moment, looking all around as though trying to recall where she'd left off. Then she turned suddenly on Leland. "Well then, why *don't* you hire her on as a hand? It sounds like it would suit you both just fine!"

Hattie and Ann arrived shortly after this. The near-frown on Ann's face changed instantly to a beautiful smile when she saw Leland.

"I brought your teapot," Leland said to Hattie, holding it out, but looking at it and not at her.

She didn't take it. Instead, she folded her arms tightly against herself as though cold. She looked older, worn out — even thinner — in the black dress.

"It's nice that you've come back," she said. "Poor Sally has been having fits with us underfoot. I'm always trying to do things one way while she does things some other way. I guess a man wouldn't understand, but it's hard for a woman used to her own home to try to live in some other woman's home without interfering. I've promised we'll move out soon."

"That's her idea," Sally put in. "As far as I'm concerned, they are welcome to stay as long as they like."

"She's so kind and good to us," Hattie said. "But it's not right for us to stay here. We're a burden to her."

"You should have heard them yesterday," Ann said to Leland. "They argued all afternoon about who ought to do the dishes. Mother said she ought to do them because she ought to do *some*thing around here, but the real reason was she didn't think some of the glasses were clean enough—"

"Ann!" Hattie said.

"So they argued about it all afternoon," Ann finished.

Sally looked flustered.

"Well then," Leland said finally, "if you're going to leave, where d'you plan to go?"

Hattie drew a deep breath.

"Leland," she said, with a meekness that made him finally look at her — and stare at her blankly while she spoke, "I really have nowhere to go but the *Harraseeket*. The *Sarah* broke up and so I have nothing from that. There's really nowhere else I could go. It would only be for a little while. I need time to get hold of things, try to forget poor Dan . . ." She swallowed, and her eyes glistened more. "I'm used to living on a schooner now, and being on shore seems complicated. I could clean and cook and wash clothes, and Ann could help out on deck, too, just like she used to help her father." Hattie paused again to swallow back tears. "We would stay out of your way."

When all was said and done, Hattie and Ann returned to the *Harraseeket*. Leland, like a hurricane, got his power from the sea, and when ashore his determination and assurance faded quickly. This, together with his promise to Dan, left him at Hattie's mercy. He was aware that there might be more to Hattie's motives than appeared on the surface, and he suspected that the new humility might not mean there would be no more of the old Hattie. But a kind of fatalism about the business had set in, and his efforts to figure a way of avoiding the return of the women aboard always deteriorated into brooding over his ill fortune.

So, the next day the *Harraseeket* went to sea with Ann happily running here and there lending a hand and Hattie below in the after cabin trying to figure out how to arrange things.

7

"I think it would be best if you and Frank moved into the forecastle," Hattie said, before they were two hours out of Port Clyde.

Leland was at the helm; Ann stood a few steps away at the weather rail, erect and proud; Frank sat up on the deckload of yellow birch flooring chewing on a strip of pollock, a dubious look on his face; and Hattie was braced in the companionway looking a bit seasick. The *Harraseeket* was plunging along, beating to windward against a brisk southwester and a chop under a cloudy sky.

"Fo'c'sle's stowage," Leland said with an air of ending the conversation.

"Well, we can't all sleep in the same cabin, can we?" Hattie said.

"Should've thought of that before you decided to go in the *Harraseeket*. I wasn't planning for no women aboard."

"Well, we're here," Hattie said. It was plain she wasn't used to the *Harraseeket*'s lively motion — it would never have done to push the old *Sarah* this way. She was hanging on tightly. "Oh Leland," she said, "I know we're a trouble and a burden to you, but once things are organized properly, it won't be so bad. You don't *really* want us in the same cabin with you, do you? You could build a partition the way Dan did . . ." she paused to swallow hard, "but that does seem like asking too much, and in the end it's still the same cabin. But if you and Frank move into the forecastle you are away from us, and from all the cooking chores, too. You can just come into the after cabin to eat."

Leland had not really thought that much about how to make the arrangement work, having spent his efforts entirely in reinforcing his conviction that the whole idea was no good and wrong, and in trying desperately to think of a quick way to unload the women. The idea of actually having to live with them aboard only now began to sink in.

"I do all my own cooking," he said curtly. "If you want to move into the fo'c'sle you're welcome."

"But why should you have to do any cooking with me here to do it for you? I will not be a charity case."

"You are just that," Leland said bluntly. "There's no point pretending about it. If you want privacy you can sleep in the fo'c'sle. That'll be all right. Frank'll help you clear some of the stowage out and find you some blankets."

Hattie looked hurt, but bowed her head and stopped arguing at this point, and she and Ann made up bunks for themselves in the forecastle. Frank talked Leland into letting the women have the straw donkey's-breakfasts to sleep on, promising to go ashore at the first opportunity and get more.

That night as they lay at anchor, Leland was awakened by the sound of the hatch sliding back.

He lay quietly back in the dark hole of his bunk, watching. Against the starry night sky he saw the lithe shape of Ann slip silently into the cabin. Her presence made him hold his breath, his stomach tight. In the unguardedness of having just awakened, the thought shot through him: Is she coming here to find me? For what? The thought actually frightened him, making his palms sweat, but a moment later he had regained his usual control and outlook. He heard her move to the galley and fumble in one of the drawers, making a low rattle of pots.

"Need something?" Leland asked, his voice low and calm. Frank's snoring continued undisturbed.

"Oh, I'm sorry," Ann said softly. "I was trying not to wake you up."

"That's all right," he said. "What do you need?"

"Mother's sick. Do you have a bowl or bucket or something? And some towels or clean rags?"

Leland got out of his bunk, pulled on his clothes in the dark, and then stepped over to the galley, Ann saying meanwhile, "Oh, don't get up, really, don't. Mother is all right. It's just leftover seasickness from today and something she ate that didn't agree with her. She never has liked fish chowder very well."

Now he stood near her in the dark, pulling towels out of a drawer, the spare cedar bucket from under the sink.

"I don't have any medicines," he said. "Never use any myself. All I have is some cotton and tape for a bad leak o' blood, and black coffee. I guess none of them is what's wanted."

"Oh, it's nothing bad," Ann said. "She doesn't have a fever or anything. You really don't have to bother to get up. You should go right back to sleep. I'll look after Mother. She'll be all right."

But Leland didn't hand over the towels or the bucket. "You get on along. I've got this stuff."

Ann paused a moment. He could just barely make her out standing close in front of him, and he wondered what she was thinking — then he wondered what *he* was thinking, up like this to worry himself over Hattie. Ann went nimbly up the companionway and onto the deckload. He followed.

Hattie had been sick on the deck just outside the forecastle companionway. She had gone around to the forward bulkhead of the forecastle and was propped against it, wrapped in a blanket, her face very pale in the starlight.

"Leland?" she said in a barely audible, piteous voice.

"Didn't like my fish chowder?" he asked her, and squatted to get a closer look at things.

"Of course I've always had a delicate stomach," she said tremulously. "And of course the poor old *Sarah* never could be sailed the way you sail your boat, so I'm not used to all that thrashing. Thank you so much for bringing the towels — Ann dear, you really didn't need to disturb Leland about me."

"Let's get you back to your bunk," Leland said. "Do you think you'll need this bucket? Never mind, I'll leave it next to your bunk anyway, so you'll have it if you want it and you won't have to come out here. I'll wash the deck."

"Well, of course if you put me back down in that dark little pigeonhole I'll be sure to need it all night," Hattie said.

What could he do after that? He woke up Frank and in the middle of the night they switched cabins, and so it remained thereafter, just as Hattie had wanted it in the first place.

She was much better by morning, and she insisted on cooking the breakfast, arguing that if she made it herself she could hardly blame Leland if she got sick again. She did not get sick.

Since she occupied the cabin where the galley was, and since both Frank and Leland were wary of simply barging into the place without being sure the ladies within were dressed and neither was making use of the cedar bucket, Hattie had not too much difficulty in arranging to have breakfast either made or well under way by the time the men were allowed in. Dinner and supper she also contrived to make while Leland and Frank were otherwise engaged, and so Hattie's desire to be cook and earn her keep also came to pass.

Whatever else he might think about Hattie, Leland did have to admit she could cook pretty well. He was not ready to admit she could cook as well as he could, but she was not so bad at it that he minded eating the meals she served. It did make some extra time for him, after all, and if he was going to have to support two women for a little while he could use it.

So he reasoned things to himself. He didn't admit the idea that there might possibly be some benefit to having a wife, nor dwell on the possibility that there might be no conscionable way to get rid of the women in the near future. Meanwhile, as a short-term method of keeping peace in the *Harraseeket*, while he thought out how to dispose of his responsibilities, he refrained from putting up a fight every time Hattie asked something of him. That was how he came to build her a bedstead, and also some curtain rods and one or two other things. These projects actually took up more time than he had gained by having the cooking chores taken off his hands, but Leland considered it a temporary situation which would not continue for too long.

When Leland laid the *Harraseeket* neatly against the wharf at Lynn where they were to unload, the schooner had about her enough change of atmosphere and aspect that interest was aroused. The company's representative was surprised to see Leland go into the forecastle to get the shipping manifest. The stevedores did not fail to take note of the curtains Hattie had put in the rectangular windows of the after cabin. Everyone wanted to know in just what capacity the women were aboard. Leland simply glared at the askers of this question, but the men smiled among themselves when Leland was not looking.

These men knew Ann and her mother from the *Sarah*'s occasional trips here, and they had learned to accept Ann's helping with unloading. But Leland had accepted nothing. Though Ann had a quiet way of being in the right place at the right time to make herself useful, and had shown herself competent to do whatever she was allowed to, Leland was still sure the moment would come when she would do something stupidly womanish. He was not about to entrust anything important to her, and he always checked whatever she did do. The only thing he ever actually asked her to do was keep out of the way. He refused her offers to take the helm, help tail away on halyards, or lend a hand during anchoring and heaving clear. He would not even let her handle dock lines. Nevertheless she persisted, and was on hand when it came time to start discharging cargo.

Under the interested eyes of the stevedores, Leland told her to go below and help her mother. She went, but returned shortly saying her mother had nothing for her to do, and did he want her to unreeve the lashings and lifelines? Leland said nothing, being in no mood to further entertain the stevedores, and so she went to work.

When she had finished with the lashings and lifelines, she put on a pair of heavy gloves and did what she could to help unload. Yellow birch is heavy even when dry, and this was still somewhat green. Though flooring is narrow, a lot of this was in long lengths, and handling it was hard work for Ann. She was not ruggedly built. Yet even so she managed to be helpful, turning boards on edge and sliding them to Leland and Frank. This speeded things up considerably once they were working below and lumber had to be brought to the hatch from the ends of the vessel.

While they were off-loading, Hattie offered to go do some shopping. "We need all kinds of things," she said.

"We ain't finished that pollock yet," Leland said. "And we've still got some pork scraps and potatoes."

"Flour and sugar are low," she said. "And we need more salt and seasonings and greens. If you just give me some money, I'll go do the shopping. It'll save you time."

Leland was reluctant, but he knew Hattie well enough to know she would make trouble if he didn't give in. So, telling himself it was to see what would happen, he gave her some money.

"This isn't nearly enough," she said, apparently surprised. "Food isn't given away, you know."

"If you know where to look, that's plenty."

"It's enough if all you eat is pollock. But it's not good for you to do that. You want to eat some other things. If I have what I need, I can make meals twice as good as the ones we've been having."

"That's twice what I usually spend," Leland said. "I'm not spending more than that."

He made it stick this time, but Hattie still spent the money as she intended, and the result was they needed to shop again much sooner than Leland had planned.

The *Harraseeket,* loaded with a varied cargo of building and other supplies for some new cottages being built at Wilson Island in Penobscot Bay, was rolling along headed down east on the breast of the prevailing southwesterly. The wind was light though, and they weren't moving very fast.

Hattie was below, as usual. Ann had out one of the *Harraseeket*'s old jibs and sat repairing it in the sunny lee of the forecastle, looking as happy as could be.

But Frank stood at the helm looking troubled. When Leland came by, Frank said, "Cap'n, I been thinking." He screwed up his face and was silent for a bit.

"Well, out with it then," Leland said.

"I was wondering," Frank said, but he stopped again, frowning. Finally he asked, "How long do you figure Hattie'll want to go in this here vessel?"

"I reckon she'll want to stay forever."

Frank looked shocked. "You mean . . . I wouldn't-a thought . . . well, that's kind of a long time, ain't it?"

"Forever is a mighty long time," Leland said, staring grimly ahead.

"Well, you know, I never signed on no vessel full of women," Frank said.

"You're damned right you didn't," Leland said with feeling.

Frank looked confused for a moment, but then he appeared to recover his train of thought, and he said, "Well, I was wondering what you aim to do about them. It just makes me awful nervous."

"Makes me more'n that. Don't you worry, I intend to get rid of these two."

"How?"

"I don't know yet, exactly. I got to figure a plan."

"Yeah," Frank said doubtfully. "Hattie has got things all her way so far, ain't she?"

"No she ain't. She just *thinks* she has, is all."

"How's that, Cap'n?"

"Well, someday she's going to get a surprise."

"It won't be easy to give Hattie no surprises," said Frank.

Leland lay awake most of that night. He saw himself pushed out of his own cabin, out of his own galley in his own vessel — curtains in the windows, by jiggers — sleeping in his own forecastle like a hired hand, jumping around making things for *Hattie* just because she asked, even giving her his own money to spend.

What the hell was happening to him? It was getting so he couldn't tell himself from a married man. He had been pretending there was a big difference, but when you came right down to it there wasn't that much.

He got about an hour of sleep before dawn, in restless snatches of five and ten minutes each, and the first thing Hattie said to him in the morning was, "You look poorly, Leland. Don't you feel well?"

They made Portland the next day, the weather being squally and spattered with short periods of blinding rain. Coasters hated to go into Portland. There was a saying that seeking refuge in that port would mean a stay of at least ten days. It was a long way in and out for an overnight stop in any case, but Leland had to go in to pick up some pieces of furniture one of the Wilson Island cottage builders wanted moved from a house there to the place he was having built on the island down east.

They loaded at one of the wharves, then towed out to anchor. Frank had been restless ever since the schooner's bow had pointed towards Portland. Now he wanted to know if he might go ashore.

"I'll be back before you need me," he said.

"Well, I guess it wouldn't do any good to stop you," Leland said. "If you ain't seen enough by now to cool you off, there ain't much hope for you."

Frank grinned at Hattie and Ann, who were standing with them on deck. "He always says something like that!" he told them. "Well, I got to go!"

Hattie was smiling. "Going to see Susanna?" she asked him.

"Well, I guess *so!*" he said, and went bounding gaily down the deck like a joyful dog.

Hattie laughed. A thought struck Leland.

"You want to go along, too?" he asked Ann.

"With *Frank?*" she asked, surprised, while Hattie simultaneously said, "A girl wandering around the docks alone at *night?*"

Then, after a moment, Hattie said, "Of course, it would be

different if you went with her. Why don't you do that — you would have a good time and it would do you both such a lot of good to get away from this old schooner."

Leland bristled at the *Harraseeket* being referred to as "this old schooner," but just now the battle was being fought at another front. "I ain't got time to go dillydallying around ashore," he said. "I was just offering Ann the chance if she wanted it, but I guess she don't, but that's all right, that's her affair."

An end was put to the discussion at this point by the pop-pop of the yawl-boat engine under the stern of the *Harraseeket*; a moment later the yawl-boat was in view, heading for shore, Frank craning eagerly forward, sitting on the edge of the thwart.

Leland started to walk away forward, wondering if he shouldn't have gone ashore himself and left the women here — but where would he go? There were too many people and nothing there he wanted anything to do with.

"Captain Wells?" Ann called.

"What's that?" he asked, half turning.

"Do you like to play checkers?"

"Oh, I don't know. I got things to do."

"Can I help?"

"No," he said, and went forward.

If he had seen the look on Ann's face after this exchange he might have felt even worse than he did already.

8

Frank was still gone when dawn arrived. Fog had settled in during the wee hours of the morning and it was the fog mull kind, lying dense and silent over the harbor, muffling sounds and limiting vision to a few feet. Water hung in rows of big droplets under booms, from every bight of rope and everywhere there was an underside to hang from. Everything was soaking wet. The big droplets would fall at deliberate intervals.

If Frank had belonged to any other schooner, his absence would have been no cause for alarm, since no one else in the harbor would leave port in a fog like this. But Leland was very apt to leave, even though there was a nearly dead calm, towing out to sea in the hope of finding some whisper of a breeze. And Frank had been going in the *Harraseeket* long enough to know this.

Leland was out on deck every few minutes for a look and a listen, and every time he went below again he was angrier. Hattie had the stove going in the after cabin to keep things drier, and on each return Leland would fiddle with the stove in some way, adjusting either the flue damper or the one on the door, or look in to see how the fire was doing. Then he would pace up and down and mutter about Frank.

"Leland," Hattie said finally — she had found some old socks of his that were full of holes and was working away darning them — "what are you so steamed up about? We're obviously not going anywhere in this fog mull, and why shouldn't the boy stay ashore and have all the time he can with Susanna? After all, he doesn't have that many chances to be with her, does he?"

"He should be back here and we should be towing out to sea," Leland said. "A little fog ain't nothing to stop at, and he knows it."

"You wouldn't go to sea in this?" Hattie was astonished.

"Well, I guess I know the way well enough by now. Some folks get all worried over a little fog, but there ain't no need of it. Hell of a sailor he makes made fast to some girlie and her notions."

"You're such a fool, Leland," Hattie said. "Haven't you ever been in love?"

"Love!" Leland glared at her. "Sthf!" he said, and went out on deck again to look for Frank, Hattie shaking her head and Ann sitting quiet and pensive in a corner.

Frank did not appear until the middle of the afternoon. By this time, Leland, who had had to wait helplessly with no way to get to shore and collar his wayward hand, was roaring mad.

"Just where in hell have you been?" Even with the fog Leland must have been heard over most of the big harbor. He stood with his feet apart and his hands on his hips, glaring as Frank came on board.

Frank had trouble getting up over the rail, and he seemed a little loose in the joints once he'd gained the deck.

He grinned foolishly. "Come for my things!" he said.

"What? You damn fool. You're hot's a red wagon. Come on and I'll get you some coffee."

"Don't want no coffee . . . no . . . I'm comin' to draw my pay . . . leavin' . . . goin' to *sea*! . . . "

Leland took him by the arm and pulled him down into the after cabin.

"Well, look at you," Hattie said in a disappointed tone.

"Pour him some coffee," Leland said. "He's no good like this."

"Well, I guess not," Hattie agreed.

Still protesting and rambling on about being a real seaman now and through with the gunkholing shore life, he was sat down and made to drink strong black coffee from the pot that always sat on the back of the stove. After a few sips, Frank suddenly began to weep. He put his face in his hands and his shoulders hunched up and down as he sobbed. Hattie looked meaningfully at Leland.

"What's the matter, dear?" she asked. "You can tell us. We're your friends."

Frank just shook his head hopelessly and went on sobbing.

"Is it something about Susanna?" Hattie asked him.

He nodded. Leland's jaw clenched so the muscles below his ears bulged. Hattie gave Leland a what-did-I-tell-you look.

"Did she break off the engagement?" Hattie asked.

"She promised . . ." Frank sputtered. "She *promised* . . . but I found her still there . . ."

"Where was that, dear?" Hattie asked.

Frank looked up startledly through puffy, reddened eyes, as though suddenly aware of Hattie's presence.

"I don't want to talk about it no more," he said. He saw the coffee and drank off the rest of it. Then, with care, he got to his feet.

"I got to think," he said as though the idea of it pained him. "I want to go forward and take a little rest, if that's all right, Cap'n."

"Well, it's too late today to go anywheres," Leland said. "You might as well sleep it off."

An hour or two later, Leland went into the forecastle and found Frank awake, struggling with his thoughts. Leland sat down and waited. Frank kept shifting around in his bunk. Leland just watched and waited.

"My head don't feel so good," Frank said in a moaning tone.

"If you didn't drink, you wouldn't have that problem," Leland said without sympathy.

"I know it," Frank said ruefully. "But I always do it anyway. I guess I ain't too smart, am I?"

"Not very."

Frank looked off into the middle distance, frowning. There was clearly something on his mind. But the silence lengthened.

"What did Susanna promise?" Leland prompted finally. "To quit Clara's?"

Frank's eyes filled again with tears.

"She promised," he said in a tone of agony.

"Women never feel obliged to keep promises that I've noticed," Leland said. "This is lucky for you, you know. You are now a free man. You've got another chance. If you have any wits you'll stay clear of women from now on."

Frank blinked at the tears and swallowed.

"I just don't understand . . ." he said. "She *promised*."

"There ain't no use trying to understand. There ain't nothing *to* understand. It's just like that with women. You were rambling before about leaving. Something about going to sea."

Frank's eyes became furtive.

"I didn't mean nothing by that," he said. He didn't meet Leland's gaze.

"You wanted to draw your pay, you said."

"I was drunk."

"You still are, mostly, crying over some slut."

Frank's hands made fists and he looked for a moment as though he might try to use them, but he settled back. He opened his mouth to say something, then changed his mind and closed his mouth again and looked away, fighting more tears.

"You got no sympathy from me on that," Leland said. "You asked for it and I tried to tell you about women. And that kind there is the worst."

Frank buried his face in the crook of his arm and rocked his head back and forth, quietly sniffing against a runny nose.

Outside there was the popping of an engine. Leland listened, heard the gentle bump as the boat came alongside, and heard the engine quit with a last cough. He left Frank still crying into his sleeve and went on deck.

"Well, how are you, Leland old man? This little gunkholer still sail good?"

Myatt Smith was a great bear of a man fifteen years younger than Leland, with a fearsome great beard and enormous seaboots into the tops of which his trousers were stuffed haphazardly. He swung easily over the rail and strode grinning towards Leland, holding out one of his huge, hairy-backed hands.

Leland didn't take the offered hand, putting his own hands on his hips and lifting his chin at Myatt in signal to him to state his business. Myatt was a man Leland could not abide.

"Well, don't be afraid of it, old man," Myatt bellowed in a boisterous, good-humored way, "even if it is twice as big as yours! There's little women that ain't afraid of it — that's the God's honest truth!" He tipped back his great shaggy head and roared up into the fog, still holding his hand out. Leland still made no move to take it, and kept his mouth firmly shut, his jaw muscles bulging at the backs of his cheeks.

By this time, Hattie and Ann had come on deck to see what was going on, and were just in view now in the foggy dusk, standing a few feet away. Hattie looked somewhat askance at the visitor. Ann unconsciously backed up against the mainmast.

Myatt evidently heard them, for he turned to look.

"Well, ain't *this* something!" he said. "I don't hardly believe it! Is this *two* women? Which one of you is his wife?"

"Neither," Leland snapped. "A friend of mine died and this is his widow and daughter. They're just here for a short while until they find a place to stay."

Myatt roared out with his big booming laugh again.

"Well, I'll be jiggered if this ain't the doggonedest thing I ever saw! You old coot you! Don't want no wife, you says! And so what does he do? Why he brings *two* women aboard without having to marry either one of them! Ain't this just slick's a schoolmarm's leg though, eh?" He laughed some more. It was a disarming and infectious laugh and seemed fairly bursting with innocent good humor. But Hattie looked put out and on the verge of saying something.

Leland was furious.

"You come here for something?" he said through his teeth.

Myatt was looking at Hattie. "Oh, don't mind me," he said entreatingly. "I don't mean nothing by my talk. Don't I know Leland would rather burn the *Harraseeket* than sail on his little round of gunkholes with a load of women aboard? He always was loyal to his friends."

Hattie opened and closed her mouth, shook her head slightly, and ended up saying nothing.

Myatt turned to Leland. "I did come for something," he said.

"Your hand Frank signed on my ship bound for Rio. I said I'd come get him off you, save you a trip taking him ashore."

"Frank!" Leland shouted. Where Myatt's voice was broad and boomed like surf on a distant beach, Leland's was hard, crackling like nearby thunder. "Get out here!"

Frank appeared, still puffy around the eyes and very reluctant. He didn't meet anybody's gaze.

"Got your bag?" Myatt asked, beaming at him like a fond father.

"You sign on his ship?" Leland asked Frank.

"Well . . ." Frank said, looking all around as though for some way out.

"Did you sign on his *ship?*"

"I guess I did."

"You *guess?*"

"Well, I believe I did."

"You *believe* you did?"

"Well, I was drunk."

"Smith here says you signed on."

"Well, then I guess I did."

"Listen," Myatt said, in a good-natured way, "there's no need of pestering the boy about it. He came out of Clara's looking mighty poorly—"

"Clara's?" Hattie asked. Frank closed his eyes and half turned away as though in anticipation of a physical blow.

"You might not know about Clara's, Ma'am, not being likely to run in that sort of society."

"Oh, I see," Hattie said, her gaze going from Frank to Leland. The look she gave Leland was one of reproach for having left her in the dark about Susanna.

"Anyway," Myatt continued, "he looked pretty bad off and so I took him to a place I know where we could get something to drink—"

"So you are responsible for that," Hattie said. She gave Myatt a cold stare.

"—and he told me all about it. Well, I been in that position more than once myself, and so I told him about one or two times — hearing how somebody else has had troubles like yours and lived through it does a world of good. I told him the best thing for him would be to go to sea, get away from hanging around here gunkholing. I got a ship that needs men, so he signed on, and that's the whole of it."

Myatt stepped over to Frank and threw a big arm around his shoulders in camaraderie.

"This here is a real seaman, I think," he said. "At least he sure can *drink* like a seaman, and there ain't no surer sign!" And he boomed out in laughter, shaking Frank roughly by the shoulders, paying no attention to Hattie's continuing cold stare.

"Frank works for me," Leland said flatly.

"Looky," Myatt said, "I know he's a good man and you hate to lose him, but going to sea'll be just the thing for him. I knew his father, and *he* was a real seaman if I ever saw one — he drunk me under the table more'n once. 'Bout time Frank saw more of the world than the little round of gunkholes you sail to. There's more girls in the world than Susanna — prettier too, eh?" He shook Frank roughly by the shoulders again and laughed. Frank looked ready to cry again, but instead managed a grin. Myatt was saying, "There's girls enough and to spare in Rio if you know where to look. Frank'll have his pick, and I'll bet pretty soon he won't miss Susanna so much. Come on, Frank, get your sea bag."

Frank looked warily at Leland, stole a terrified glance at Hattie, then made for the forecastle, returning with his bag over his shoulder and a strained smile on his face. He studied the deck self-consciously.

Leland reached into his pocket and pulled out a roll of paper money. Everybody watched as he peeled off Frank's pay and handed it to him.

"You change your mind, you look for the *Harraseeket*," Leland said.

Frank nodded awkwardly, stepping from one foot to the other as he took his pay. Leland got out another five-dollar bill.

"You've been a good hand, Frank," he said. "Sorry to see you go." Frank looked chagrined and uncomfortable, but Leland made him take the money. "You earned it," he said.

"Goodby, Frank," said Ann. She smiled her quick smile at Frank, but Frank didn't look at her. Myatt did though, and for a moment there may have been a flicker of interest aroused. At his glance, her smile faded and she pressed back against the solidity of the mainmast, shoulders lifting forward.

Then Myatt and Frank went over the side and off into the fog.

They were no sooner out of sight than Leland strode forward and began heaving short his anchor. He'd had about all he could stand of Portland.

9

Leland ran into trouble when he tried to find a new hand. The whole coast was a community, where news and gossip traveled quickly to every remote corner. Everyone knew that Leland Wells was one of the most successful coastermen, so getting a new hand should not have been a problem. But people had also heard about Hattie, and it was commonly thought that she had been skipper of Dan's schooner in fact if not in name. Word of her and Ann taking over the after cabin of Leland's schooner and driving him into the forecastle had also gotten around, and few were willing to crew on a vessel of that kind.

After off-loading at the island, Leland went into Rockland to try to get somebody. One likely looking fellow said, "Naw, I'd *like* to, but I met Hattie once." Another said, "I never took orders from no woman yet, and I don't plan to start now — no offense, Cap'n." It did no good to tell them that he gave the orders — they didn't believe this would stop Hattie from giving orders of her own.

Leland had always been unsociable, not taking much time for visiting or gamming, always anchoring at a distance from other schooners if possible. This aloofness, together with his apparent success, nearly complete self-sufficiency, and the general lack of information about his personal life, had left gossipers with little to say about him. He was generally thought to have sacks of money hidden away somewhere, and there was occasionally that speculation about what he might be saving up for, but no new grist for the gossip mill had appeared for years. Leland's life rolled on like it was all an easy scud to leeward for him, nobody ever catching him doing anything the slightest bit out of the ordinary. The man didn't touch liquor, didn't gamble, was never seen talking to any woman — or man either — that there wasn't an obvious necessity for him to speak to. He was seldom talked about at all except on the occasions when some reputedly fast schooner challenged him, usually losing. Then all the common knowledge about Leland was mentioned, and the conversation would trail off, everybody feeling the lack of any real understanding of what made the man what he was. Then some other subject would be raised and Leland forgotten.

But the advent of Hattie and Ann aboard the *Harraseeket* had changed all this. Suddenly Leland appeared to be human like anyone else. Various versions of how it was that the women went in the *Harraseeket* were discussed at gam sessions the length of the Maine coast.

Of course, people knew about Dan Procter's death and their rescue, and they mostly all sort of knew that Leland must have promised Dan he'd look after the welfare of the women, and that this must be much against the grain with Leland. Nobody seriously thought anything improper could possibly be going on — Leland being displaced from his own cabin was seen as proof enough of that. Maine people are not normally cruel in their gossip, and most of the jokes about Leland and his "floating hen coop" were good natured. But Leland's awesome self-sufficiency was galling, and this opportunity to have some fun out of the nearest thing Leland was likely to get to a comeuppance was too good to be missed.

Leland returned from his trip ashore empty-handed and in a foul mood, aware only that Hattie's presence aboard put the attractiveness of his schooner as a place to work about on a par with that of the slowest, leakiest, old run-out kiln-wooder in the fleet.

"Well, it isn't the end of the world," Hattie said, waving a spatula at him as she cooked dinner. "You know, Leland, you really ought to be grateful you have Ann."

"I'll tell you something," Leland said with considerable warmth. "If I didn't have either one of you, I'd still have Frank. He never did like the idea of women aboard. He says it's bad luck — you know the saying. And on top of that, there was Susanna and what you'd have to say to him about that piece of foolishness, and about his drinking, too."

"Now, how can you think such a thing! Of *course* he was upset about Susanna. But if *you* had had a kind word to say to him, instead of always telling him what a fool he was, maybe he would have stayed. He liked going in the *Harraseeket*. He told me that himself. Don't try to tell *me* he left just because of that old superstition. That Smith man tried to cheer him up, and did it, too. You could have done that, and without liquor either, but you didn't. Well, it's done now. You ought to be grateful for what you have. Ann is always willing to help, and she can steer and help pull up sails and a lot of other things, too, if you'd let her."

"All I told Frank was the truth, but let it go. I guess it's no use telling some how things are. They just ain't made to hear it."

"You want to hear some truth? You just pay a little attention to Ann and you'll find out she's more use and help than you think."

"Ann is all right," Leland admitted. "But she ain't a man."

"Well," Hattie said, turning away from him to hide a sly smile, "that's very true. She sure ain't a man."

Leland pondered Hattie's broad back trying to figure out why she seemed to think he had yielded a point to her.

A day or two later, the *Harraseeket* was wafting into a tiny cove not far from Sorrento, in Sullivan Harbor, on the last of the breeze, the sun low over Crabtree Neck behind them. The mouth of the cove was only yards wide, and the channel lay hard against the northern shore, which was rocky with a dark wall of spruce coming right to the water's edge. They glided over clear water, smooth as glass except for little patches of tiny ripples that came and went with the dipping of the faint breath of air to the surface. What breeze there was puffed haphazardly around within the cove's walls of spruce like a spirit flitting about from shore to shore announcing the schooner's arrival. The *Harraseeket*'s sails barely registered the movements of the spirit, hanging heavily limp and useless. The schooner moved almost entirely on her own way, once in the cove, gliding in majestic silence towards the rickety pole wharf that ex-tended the few yards from a hole in the spruce wall to a point just beyond the last rock visible above water.

The steering gear creaked slightly, and the schooner turned, moving ever more slowly, and with the last vestige of her way bumped gently against the pole wharf. Ann hopped nimbly over the side and made fast the lines. There was only the sound of a squirrel whirring somewhere nearby. All around was the smell of the spruces, and in powerful whiffs as the air currents of the place shifted, the smell of new-sawn wood.

"Now, you're not going to insult Ann by jumping over and fretting about her knots, are you?" Hattie said to Leland.

Leland shook his head with a hint of impatience. Ann gave him a brief but penetrating examination before swinging back over the rail to stand beside him, looking into the woods.

"Isn't it beautiful here?" she said softly.

"I hope this fellow looked at the bottom before he built that wharf," Leland said. "Some of 'em never stop to think about what a schooner will sit on when the tide goes out."

Ann leaned over the rail and peered down into the clear water. "What I can see looks good."

"Well, we got to find this fellow and ask him."

Hattie started making supper and Leland, with Ann pacing along proudly at his side, went into the hole in the woods and along the raw trail. The thick layer of needles had been mixed up with the dark earth underneath, and here and there the bark was rubbed off a tree root, revealing the yellow surface of the sapwood. They rounded a bend not fifty yards from the shore and came upon a portable sawmill set up in a little clearing, a pile of sawdust to one side. The tangy smell of new-sawn wood was strong. Thousands of board feet of green lumber were neatly piled on scoots lined up ready to be hauled to the shore, and thousands more were stacked to one side. But there was no one around.

Trails led off this way and that through the woods.

"Don't hear anything," Leland said. "Must be a shack around someplace."

They found the shack, a crude structure made of low-grade boards. The floor was dirt, the stove an ancient potbellied affair with a few lengths of rusty stovepipe to send the smoke outdoors. The shack's door stood open, but there was nobody here either.

Then as they started back for the mill, they heard a shout, and out of the woods strode two rugged-looking men in heavy boots and patched clothing. One appeared about forty, the other something less than twenty. They both had shotguns in the crooks of their arms, and the younger carried a dead domestic chicken in the other hand.

"You a schoonerman?" the older man asked.

"That's right. I heard you had some lumber down here bound up to the west'ard."

"Jones Lumber in Boston will buy all I can cut."

"I can start loading first thing in the morning," Leland said. "Unless I can't stay to the wharf. You build that wharf?"

"Sure did."

"You happen to notice what the bottom looked like there?"

"There weren't no rocks nor laydge nor nothing like that, if that's what you're thinkin' of. I built one not regardin' that one time and one of them old lumber droghers opened up her bottom on a laydge and it was two weeks before we could get her tight enough to sail. Weren't that fellow madder'n tunket though.

"Say, my name is Mike Olson and this is my son Jack. Our team is up to a farm about two miles from here. We'll get 'em down tomorrow and start haulin'. We'd give you something to eat, but we wasn't plannin' for no company." He grinned. "We didn't bag that chicken the way you might think. We was up seeing to our hosses and Mrs. Bucklin seen our guns and asked if we'd got anything and we said no, so she said take a chicken, so we done it. We got some beans left, but I guess Jack'll clean up most of the chicken and most of the beans and I'll have to do with what's left."

"I'm Ann and this is Captain Leland Wells."

Both Mike and Jack had given Ann occasional curious glances as though not quite sure what to make of her. She had her hair all up under her slouch hat and was wearing her usual baggy men's clothing. In the dimness of the woods with the sun now down it would take a careful look to be sure she wasn't just a very delicately built boy. Once she spoke there was of course no doubt, and both woodsmen looked uncomfortable; possibly they were trying to recall if they'd said anything that shouldn't be said in the presence of women.

"See you at dawn," Leland said, and he and Ann went back to the schooner.

Loading got under way around eight o'clock in the morning. The lumber was spruce, in fairly long lengths, mostly two-inch plank — two-by-eights, two-by-tens, two-by-twelves. Even though spruce is not as heavy as some other woods, Ann was not really up to keeping pace with the men. Mike and Jack were big and strong, and all they had ever done was muscle logs and lumber around. Jack especially was like an eager dog, full of energy and perhaps some desire to show off a bit. Spending most of his life working in the woods didn't give him much chance to show pride in what he knew how to do. Mike and Jack passed the lumber over the rail, and Ann and Leland stowed it. But even though Leland had great strength and nearly endless stamina, and even though Ann struggled on with all the determination she could muster — which was considerable — they simply couldn't keep up with the woodsmen. This was partly because the load had to be stowed, and Leland was fussy about how this was done. He wanted the load both balanced and tightly packed with hardly a square inch anywhere of waste space. He insisted on doing the stowing personally.

As the day wore on, the slow pace of loading slowed still further as Ann tired. Unless he climbed out on deck to help her with every plank, there wasn't much Leland could do, so he had more and more time to stand around watching Ann's struggles and think to himself: The women have got to go, they have got to *go*.

During the next few days as they slowly worked at loading the *Harraseeket*, he turned over in his mind the idea he and Frank had talked about back a ways — getting Ann married off. Nobody was likely to marry Hattie, but with Ann there might be a chance.

He thought about Ann. She was perhaps different from other women. Unlike other women, she seemed to be reasonably sensible. And she was actually a help sailing the *Harraseeket*; even though the *Harraseeket* was a hand-puller and demanded great strength in the crew, she still managed to find a lot of chores she could handle. There might be some man who, though foolish enough to want to get married, was still smart enough to at least pick a girl with some sense and usefulness about her. And there weren't so many women you could say that about. In fact, Ann was the only one he'd ever run across.

The more he thought it over, the more reasonable the idea seemed, notwithstanding the dark cloud in the back of his mind which was made up of deep suspicions that Ann's femaleness would one day out and reveal her to be no different from the rest, together with a rebellion against the idea of trying to saddle some poor fellow with a wife when it was not something he'd want done to him.

In the end, business won out over conscience. Leland began to size up Jack Olson. Jack didn't say much, but he was a hard worker and this was enough by itself to endear him to Leland's heart. He was not a drinker — unusual for a woodsman. The only thing that seemed to be against him was that he couldn't read or write to amount to anything, and he couldn't do anything with numbers at all. Still, that could be fixed up perhaps.

Leland thought over ways to promote this business he had in mind and characteristically decided on a direct route. The *Harraseeket* was in need of having her water barrels filled, and there was a spring not too far off in the woods which the Olsons were using. So, Leland asked for Jack's help and they went to the spring carrying a pair of buckets each.

When they reached the spring, Leland said, "Are you a man who wants a wife?"

Jack had a way of straightening, putting his hands on his hips, tucking his chin in and looking thoughtfully wise when asked something that took him some thought to answer, and he did this now.

"Well, I reckon," he said finally.

"Ann would make a good wife. She has got more sense than any ten other females you might run acrost. If a man is going to marry, he ought to at least find himself a woman who has some sense and is some use to him. Otherwise he'll come to regret getting married sooner or later."

"Well, I guess," Jack said uncertainly.

"Now of course Ann ain't as strong as a man and you don't want to count on her for too much heavy work — you seen this already. But still, she is more use than most. And if a man has decided himself to get married, he might as well get something more than expense and troubles. Ann ain't like most women. She don't cost an awful lot to keep. She don't wear nothing but sensible clothes and she don't have more of them than a man does. She ain't always wanting you to spend money on her at every turn. And she don't talk and chatter on all the time either, which ain't common in a woman."

Jack filled his buckets. He didn't know a lot, but when he'd consulted the small store of his knowledge and made up his mind about something, he knew what he thought without equivocation.

"I don't want no wife that don't look like a woman or act like one," he said. And that was the end of that.

After this, Leland's mood changed. His opinion of Jack Olson went way down. Having the good sense he'd lavished rejected so bluntly and pointedly by someone he'd taken such care to build up a high opinion of annoyed him no end. It was a turning point in his approach to the problem. Whereas he had before been at war only with the female sex, he was now at war also with those men who could be attracted by all he disliked about the female sex.

By the time they had finished loading and put to sea, a new notion had occurred to Leland which he turned over and over all the way to Boston. All the while he was turning it over, he observed Ann narrowly, taking in her every word and mannerism. Of course, he couldn't watch her without having her around him, and not quite consciously this led to his letting her do many things he never had before. The opportunity to show how competent she was at a whole range of duties, from steering when the schooner danced in lively fashion over a hubbly sea, to sheeting in a big jib at the right moment when tacking in half a gale — together with Leland's sudden willingness to play checkers almost every night — made Ann full of smiles.

Hattie looked on with a singular lack of surprise and very little comment, for her. She seemed to assume Leland's new acceptance of Ann was the beginning of romance.

But Leland didn't bother himself about what Hattie thought. On the night they reached Boston, he made his first move.

"You ain't going to do no more unloading," he said to Ann, as they sat over another game of checkers. "It ain't the right work for a girl." He watched her closely as he spoke.

She goggled at him, openmouthed. Hattie looked up from her knitting.

"But I've always helped with the loading and unloading," Ann said.

"Well, you're through with it now. And with every other kind of man's work, too. I've done quite a bit of thinking on the matter and my mind's made up."

"But who's going to help you?" Ann asked.

"That ain't for you to worry about. I'll collar somebody to help me out sooner or later. Meantime I'll just have to do it all myself. You ought to be thinking about getting married, and you ain't going to find nobody going around dressed like a man and doing man's work."

"I don't believe I'm hearing what I'm hearing coming out of your mouth, Leland Wells," Hattie said, but she didn't seem in the least displeased.

"You go up into town here and buy yourself some dresses and all such as women wear," Leland went on to Ann, ignoring Hattie. "I'll give you some money, and if you need more you be sure to ask for it. From now on you wear a dress and behave like a lady."

Ann had looked betrayed and indignant at first, but now she studied Leland's face thoughtfully. Finally her face softened and she smiled and cast down her eyes and said, "All right."

"Well, I'll be!" Hattie exclaimed. "*I* never could get her to wear a dress." Ann looked momentarily irked.

"But I don't want to go all alone," Ann said to Leland. "Will you come with me?"

Leland shifted uncomfortably in his chair. "I won't have no

time for that. Anyway, I don't know nothing about things like that. Maybe your mother will go with you. She'll know more about it than I would."

"Never mind," Ann said. "I don't need her help. Should I go tomorrow?"

"Just as soon as you can," Leland said, getting up from the table.

"Aren't you going to finish the game?"

"I got to do some things." He started for the companionway.

"Well, isn't that the most amazing thing," Hattie said in a smilingly thoughtful way.

As he stepped out on deck, Leland muttered to himself, "Never expected nothin' else." But the image of Ann smiling and casting down her eyes stayed with him, making him irritable and bitter.

10

Ann was gone all morning. She returned for dinner with some packages, looking excited, but she said very little. Leland asked if she needed more money, and, with melting eyes, she accepted some. Then after dinner she went off again, still dressed in her men's clothes.

Leland was occupied with unloading, but he had watched her carefully as they ate dinner, and he thought about her all day. Until now he'd been unaware that a nearly comfortable relationship had developed between Ann and himself since they'd left Sullivan Harbor. He thought of how well they worked together tailing onto a halyard without getting in each other's way, and of the ingenious ways she managed to do things that her light weight and lack of great strength should have prevented her doing. He had begun to think of her as almost a friend, a reliable help in running the schooner, who demanded nothing in return.

But now she was about to join the ranks of the enemy — the unreliable, frivolous, manipulating, irritating, demanding bundle of contradictions and uselessness that was womankind. And what shook him was how small a push it had taken — she'd hardly put up a fight at all. This vindicated his convictions about women, but there was no satisfaction in that.

Well, it was better to have it found out. If Ann really was the same as all the rest, then he needn't bother his conscience over the plan he had to get rid of her and her mother.

Ann did not come back from her second shopping foray until late in the afternoon. Leland glanced at her, saw the soft, anxious largeness of her eyes, and looked away. He kept his attention elsewhere until he was certain she'd gotten below. Some minutes later, he was still aware of the beating of his heart.

After finishing work that day, Leland sat in the forecastle and stared at the bulkhead, rubbing his chin. He decided he shouldn't just go into the after cabin unannounced looking for supper, as he had been in the habit of doing lately. He sat on for some time, full of troubled thoughts, the oil lamp turned low.

There was a tapping on the companionway slide and a tremulous voice he did not at first recognize as Ann's said, "Captain Wells?" Usually in this situation she would tap and then sing out in a cheery, musical tone, "Supper's on!"

Leland was absolutely still for some moments, except for the beating of his heart; then he set his jaw and rose to his feet with the same aspect as that of a mighty whale rising to the surface of the sea, shedding a great wash of water. He had come to the surface out of necessity, but he expected to go down to safe depths again as soon as he'd done what he'd come up for.

He went up the steps of the companionway and stepped out on the deck. For a moment he thought he was alone and he looked quickly around.

Then he saw her. His jaw dropped and he sucked in a sharp breath.

She stood backed against the bulwark, her hands on the rail. It was now dark, but there was light enough from the sky full of stars and the crescent moon to make a magical sight of Ann in her sweeping white gown. For the first time, her long brown hair was mostly in sight, arranged so a great deal of it flowed down onto her shoulders while the rest was arranged on top of her head under a hat that contrasted starkly with the hat she normally wore. Her surprisingly thin arms were bare, and her small waist and full bosom were shown off to their best effect.

Leland had been bracing himself all day, but against the *idea* of Ann showing her femininity, not the fact of it. The fact of it caught him off guard. He had not thought at all about what she might look like, and if he had he would not have expected anything half as dramatic.

For some moments they looked at each other across the little distance, both of them frightened and at a loss as to how to behave. Finally, Ann said very softly, "It's time to eat supper."

"Well then, let's go," he said in a thick voice.

With care, she pushed away from the bulwark and walked next to him along the deck. He smelled perfume.

"So what do you think of *that!*" Hattie exclaimed to Leland as Ann preceded him down into the after cabin. Hattie's eyes were shining.

In the comparatively bright light of the lantern, Ann could be seen to be either feverish or blushing furiously. She carried herself with cautious pride.

"She's a lady now, Leland," Hattie said. "It took a man to bring it out in her — you. Now hold that chair for her."

This irritated Leland and partially brought him back to normal. He gave Hattie an annoyed look.

"If she's going to be a lady," Hattie said with an attitude of utter reasonableness, "she's got to know what to expect from men who will treat her like a lady. So help her out and hold the chair."

Leland hated to admit it, but, with what he had in mind for Ann, Hattie's advice made sense. He held the chair. Ann swept up her skirts and carefully sat down. Leland helped her move the chair in, and then she carefully arranged her skirts. Hattie looked on shrewdly, smiling. Leland stepped away and around the table to the other side, aware that he felt warm.

"So, you still haven't told me what you think of our blossoming lady here," Hattie said to Leland, when she had served up the meal and they were about to start eating.

Leland felt Ann's eyes on him, but he didn't look at her.

"I guess it's better than looking like a man, if she is going to find somebody to marry her."

"Well! Isn't that a compliment?" Hattie laughed. "Come, come, Leland, you can do better than that. Do you think she's pretty?"

"Please, Mother," Ann pleaded in a strained voice.

"Well, he ought to at least admit that much," Hattie said.

Leland managed to avoid looking at Ann during the rest of the meal, but when he got up to escape to the forecastle, Hattie said sharply, "Aren't you forgetting something, Leland?"

When he glanced around, his eye fell on Ann sitting blushing, staring into her empty plate with her hands tightly holding each other in her lap. For some moments he couldn't take his eyes off her.

"Her chair, Leland," Hattie said gently.

He looked blankly at Hattie, and she beamed at him.

"Oh, you're a goner, I can see that!" she said gaily.

It took Leland all night to get hold of himself. He slept not at all. But as the first light of dawn began to creep into the forecastle he was very nearly his old self, and neither the great wrestlings he'd been through nor the lack of sleep prevented him from going on deck with his usual springy step for an eager look at the weather. It seemed to be making up to be a fairly good day, though it was only an unloading day and the weather didn't matter so much.

A moment after his habitual look at the weather, he noticed Ann sitting on the edge of the open main hatch. She was back in her usual men's clothes. Though in a way this was a great relief to Leland, it was also an unpleasant surprise.

"Morning," he said to her, cautiously, coming nearer.

"Good morning," she said timidly, looking up at him.

"Something wrong?" he asked, noting the expression on her face.

"I don't know," she said. "I was just thinking about things." She sounded wistful. She stood up. "I don't know if I like dressing up that way," she said. "I keep catching a dress on everything, and I feel so foolish having somebody hold my chair for me and all that. It just doesn't seem natural. But are you angry at me for saying that? Is that what you really like? I mean, I never saw you look at me like that before! But it was like you were afraid to come anywhere near me, like I had smallpox or something, and I like . . . I don't want . . . oh, I don't know, I've never been so mixed up in my life."

By morning, Leland had resettled everything in his mind and calculated to go ahead with his plan for Ann. But he hadn't figured on her reacting like this. He'd thought once the cat was let out of the bag, that was it. Now what? *Was* Ann at least a little different from other girls? He had never heard of another girl who felt uncomfortable wearing a dress. How did she think he'd looked at her, anyway? The hell with that.

"Suppose you tell me something," he said. "Do you ever want to get married?"

She looked at him quickly, then away. "I might if I was asked."

"Well then," Leland said determinedly, "if you want to be asked, you've got to look like a woman and act like a woman and *think* like a woman. Most men aren't sensible like me and they want wives. But they ain't wanting *use*fulness in a wife, or good sense, as far as I can see. They want femaleness. So, if you want to get men interested in you, you can't go around looking like a man or working like one, because that ain't what the average man is looking for when he's looking for a wife."

Ann smiled up at him and asked whimsically, "But you are not the average man looking for a wife?"

"Not hardly."

"Tell me what Mr. Average Man is like."

Leland felt a little irritated with her. Here he was trying to be serious and tell her things for her own good . . . well, it wasn't *only* for her own good — but if she wanted to get married, this was the only way to do it, wasn't it?

Looking at her smiling playfully at him, he had a sudden vivid memory of how she had looked the night before, and to put it out of his mind he began to talk.

"The average man," he said, "ain't got no control of what he thinks or feels or wants. He thinks if he gets married all his problems will be solved, and even if he had sense enough to see this ain't really going to be so, he *hasn't* got sense enough to stay away from women, never mind he knows well enough they are his weakness . . . "

"And what kind of women does he like?" She was fairly bubbling over with amusement.

"Just the one kind there is: vain, ignorant, foolish, helpless, squeamish, underhanded. She'll run his life for him, and some men never seem to even notice she's doing it. They think they're running their own ship."

"And you want to make me like that?" She clapped her hands and danced around in delight. "I don't even know how to begin!"

"Then I'll tell you how," he plunged on, headlong. "If you pay attention you'll be able to go ashore on Wilson Island and take your pick of the rich rusticators there."

"And once I've taken my pick of these rich men, what do I do then?"

"You marry him, of course," Leland said quite seriously.

Ann laughed merrily and danced off down the deck. Leland, sweating, watched her go. He didn't know what to make of her reaction to his plan, but he was determined to see she went ashore at Wilson Island a lady.

He didn't try to say anything more to her until after they had left Boston and were at sea. Ann had not dressed up again in that time, but neither had she tried to help with the unloading of the lumber or the loading of more furniture destined for Wilson Island. She watched Leland with a kind of secret little smile, and though she still wore her men's clothes she did so in a way that was calculated to contrast them with herself rather than as camouflage. Hattie seemed on edge and kept trying to pry information out of Leland and Ann, but they kept their mouths shut. They did not play checkers, either, while in port; Leland worked long hours and spent most of his spare time sleeping.

But once at sea, sliding along down east on a fitful damp southerly under an overcast sky and over oily swells, Leland called Ann aft to the helm.

"Take her along a little," he said.

Ann stepped immediately and confidently to the big wheel and glanced aloft at the sails with a practiced eye.

"*No!*" he said emphatically, and she looked at him startled.

"No woman out to interest the marrying kind would do like that," he said. "You want to come over all timid and uncertain and make out that you don't know anything about sailing a schooner. Now try it again." He took the wheel from her.

"If I'm going to do that," she said mischievously, "I ought to be dressed up, shouldn't I?" She watched him with a teasing smile.

"Probably you should," he agreed. "But you don't want anything to happen to your fancy clothes, do you? Why don't you pretend."

"I have more than one dress, you know."

"Save them for Wilson Island."

"Are you afraid you'll fall in love with me?" she asked, and it was hard to tell how seriously she meant the question.

"Don't ask foolish questions. I'm just trying to tell you how to behave if you want to snag one of these rich rusticators."

"I'm sorry," she said, but she was smiling at something.

"Do you want to get married or don't you?" he asked her, frowning.

"I don't know. Maybe I'm like you — too sensible to get married."

"Well then, there's nothing I can do," he said coldly. "Here," he added, offering the wheel, and she took it soberly.

The rest of that day he treated her as he had before opening this rough stretch of feminine waters. She helped on deck with her usual competence and seemed thoughtful. But nothing was the same now, and the more he turned things over in his mind the more irritable and disgusted he became. That night after supper when Ann asked if he wanted to play checkers, he said no. He went to the forecastle intending to take a squeaky halyard block apart, grease it and restrop it, and then go to bed.

He had gotten the old strop off and was about to drive the pin out of the block when there was a tap at the open companionway. It was a hot night and the forecastle was a close place in the heat.

"Can I come in, Captain Wells?" Ann asked. He glanced up, but the lantern was between him and the companionway so he couldn't see anything.

"All right," he said. And the next he knew there was Ann in her gown and very feminine hat.

He was like an animal that stares into the light and can't look away.

"May I sit down?" she asked at length.

"Oh," he said, "sure. Go ahead, if you want." But she remained standing before him, eyes cast modestly down, coloring prettily.

"Oh," he said, and got up and stepped carefully around her to the old chair he'd brought from the after cabin when he moved into the forecastle. He moved it forward and she alighted on the chair like a butterfly. Her fragrance, delicate as it was, overcame the pervasive smells of linseed oil and pine tar. Standing over her, his breath came short. Her hair was drawn back and rolled on the back of her head, but some longish stray hairs fell whimsically away from the rest at her neck. What he saw beyond that he didn't want to think about. He closed his eyes and stepped deliberately back from her, and then sidled around to his previous seat on an apple crate, where the block lay on top of a battered seaman's chest before him. He picked up the hammer and pin punch again.

"What do you want?" he asked, when he thought he could speak normally.

"I've come for my lessons," she said. "I'll be good this time." She sat primly with her hands folded in her lap.

– 130 –

He concentrated on the block for a few moments and got the pin out, and the sheave, and looked them over — they were all right.

"I ain't really no expert on such things," he said. "All I can do is tell you what you got to be like to be womanish, and you'll have to study out how to do it exactly, by yourself. I reckon you'll find it comes naturally enough. First thing to remember is to seem ignorant about everything, especially schooners. Don't let on to know anything about anything. What you got to do is let men do everything for you and tell them whatever they want to hear; and when you want something, don't try to get it for yourself or do it for yourself. Always get a man to do it for you, and make him think there ain't nobody else on earth who could do it for you but him. What you want to do is talk all about how much you want whatever it is, and all about how impossible it would be for you to do it or get it or make it yourself, being only a woman, and these fellows of the marrying kind will fall all over themselves to do the thing for you."

Leland paused and took up a gub of tallow and started rubbing it on the pin. Out of the corner of his eye he saw Ann's slim hands slowly smoothing her dress, and the thought crossed his mind that they did look more in place doing that than they ever had trying to help work timber into the hold of the *Harraseeket* — it seemed a wonder she could have been any use at all at that.

"Now, once you've got one of these fellows to do something for you, you can't leave well enough alone. You have to tell him that you are so sorry, but it turns out it wasn't really just what you wanted after all. And you think up something *else* for him to do for you. And you got to keep this up or he'll lose interest. Mind, I don't claim to understand this business, but I'm telling you what I seen happen. This world is a funny place and everything in it seems so natural and sensible until you look close.

"Now, some other things. To keep one of these fellows interested, you got to complain all the time about how ugly you are and how you wish this wasn't wrong with you and that wasn't, and you got to keep this up until you fetch a compliment out of him. And you got to *keep* making him tell you how pretty you are, even if you already know you are, or he might look for some other woman who *will* make him say it over and over. And whenever you go someplace, you want to be late. You got to always be keeping him waiting, never mind if it makes any sense or not. Sometimes you got to complain you got a headache and not show up at all, especially if you've kept him waiting a long time already. And when you have to make a decision about something, you want to take as long as you can to make up your mind, and make it as full of agony for him as you can until he's fairly ready to die if only you'd make up your mind, and then as soon as you do make up your mind you want to change it right off. The main thing to remember is to be as useless and helpless and underhanded as you can and make sure a fellow hasn't got no time to consider his wits or good sense for waiting on and paying attention to you. The average man gets married out of *weak*ness, not out of good sense, and so you can't afford to give him any chance to consider what he's about. If you do want to get married, you'll come to understand all this better than I do. You're a woman all right, so that means you'll figure it out pretty good soon enough."

There was a long silence. Leland hadn't looked at her since getting the inadvertent glimpse of her hands smoothing her dress, and he wasn't about to look at her now. He concentrated on his work on the block. That block gave him a sense of orientation and perspective. It put him in mind of all the hours he'd spent building the *Harraseeket*, the repairs he'd done, the way she flew over the water; and to work on the block was to be constantly reminded of the joy his schooner gave him. It made it possible for him to think clearly and rise above the influence of Ann's powerful attractions.

He continued to work on the block during the long silence, seizing on the strop, his hands dark with pine tar, the smell of it now stronger where he was than Ann's delicate perfume. For him it was almost a comfortable silence, with the block to work on.

"You know," Ann said earnestly, "I'm so glad you aren't the average man who wants a wife."

11

Wilson Island, heavily wooded and of about ninety acres, is located on the east side of Penobscot Bay, south of Deer Isle. A few steep little gravel beaches are tucked in protected places, but otherwise the shore is naked granite. There is one cove, opening in a southeasterly direction, which is usually a fairly snug harbor, though it has a bad reputation for bores in an extended northeaster. It's called Jettison Cove, and the story is that a pirate named Low dumped treasure overboard here to keep it out of the hands of a mutinous crew, though no treasure has ever been found.

In this cove there was, in the summer of 1905, a well-cared-for dock with gasoline and naphtha available to club members. Tied to the dock was a long, sleek, dark-hulled, naphtha launch, all polished brass fittings and varnished mahogany. She had a long, low cabin with curtains in the windows and could move along at a respectable eight knots. She looked self-consciously modern, not having even stumpy masts. There was an old retired sea captain hired to look after the launch and run her. He lived in a little neat house just up the bank from the dock and had charge also of running the flag up and down the pole next to the house. Moored out from the dock were several small sailboats and one bigger one. Dinghys and some elegant little rowing boats were tied up opposite the launch's berth.

The sun was hot the August morning the *Harraseeket* sailed into the little cove. Well-kept and graceful as she was, she still looked awkwardly big and plain beside the Wilson Island boats. Where most of them had varnish, the *Harraseeket* had paint, or oil and Stockholm tar. Leland was sensitive to this and it made him take excessive pride in the working nature of his schooner. There was not a lot of dock space aft of the launch, but that didn't bother Leland at all in his nearly belligerent mood. He bore down on the dock under full sail, boxhauled the *Harraseeket* around and dropped her gently into place a couple of feet away from the launch's varnished transom. The *Harraseeket*'s long main boom extended several feet out over the launch's after deck. Leland didn't even let on to notice the existence of the launch. He performed the whole maneuver single-handed, including the dock lines, having pointed out that if Ann were going to go ashore a convincing lady she could hardly reveal herself the same drab deckhand she had been on the previous visit here. He wanted her to say she came from Boston and not admit to knowing anything about schooners.

She had gone along with this and was on deck, wearing one of the new dresses, to watch Leland show the Wilson Islanders how a real schoonerman docks his vessel. And when he had casually finished making fast the last dockline — some Wilson Island Clubbers watching with awe — she danced up and down like a little girl and clapped her hands in delight. She was in a fever of excitement about going ashore all dressed up. The truth was she had discovered her vanity and was not yet certain how she ought to deal with it.

The lame old ship captain came down from the house and stood admiring the *Harraseeket* and allowed as how he'd seen prettier handling of vessels in his time — but not often. He also spent some time admiring Ann, which made her blush.

It was not long before word of the pretty Boston lady's arrival spread throughout the island's population — perhaps it took an hour to reach the secluded cottages on the far end of the island. Nobody ever asked what had become of the deckhand. Some of the first people to arrive at the dock invited her up to stay at their cottages or to have dinner with them. Ann was a little flustered at all the attention and she looked questioningly at Leland. He nodded at her to go ahead, and she went off up the little hill with a group of admirers.

Most of the Wilson Island summer people had been coming there for years. They were doctors, lawyers, reasonably successful businessmen, a college professor or two, with their wives and children. These children were mostly grown now, with children of their own. Not all of them kept coming to Wilson Island, however, so there was a preponderance of older people, which gave the place a somewhat staid atmosphere. The men rowed about a little or went sailing. On days of very moderate wind even some of the oldest men went sailing, and took their wives. There were walks and, among the older generation, walking sticks. There were picnics at various favorite places along the shore. Some went swimming — well covered up, of course. There were rocking chairs and hammocks on verandas, swing chairs on lawns. The cottages were typical of the type anywhere in Maine: white with green shutters, perhaps some scalloped shingles in the peaks painted red to set them off, no cellar, bare studs inside, unpainted walls sporting colored lithographs, the furnishings generally retirees from the town house. Black iron sinks, cast-iron wood stoves, floors covered with straw matting. Nowadays, visitors to Maine were being referred to more and more as summer people, or summer complaint, but to Leland they were still rusticators.

It being still an hour short of noon, Leland began unloading immediately. He got some help from the two workmen hired to build the new cottage the load of furnishings was for. This was the third cottage they had built here this summer, and they were full of talk about how some of the old guard didn't like the new building going on, while others were happy to have some of the children decide to stay, instead of building on the main.

Ann didn't return until evening, and when she did, she was escorted by a young, weak-chinned fellow in a suit and a level-brimmed straw hat. He stopped with her on the dock a distance from the schooner and seemed to be in earnest conversation with her — that is, he was talking earnestly and she was listening. Leland didn't let on to be much interested in the pair as he went about dipping up buckets of salt water and sluicing down the deck to keep it swelled tight. It gave him an odd feeling to see her that way, dressed up and talking to some unknown boy, but if he had any misgivings he kept them well stowed under battened hatches.

Hattie came on deck and stood watching the pair with one hand to her throat. Leland couldn't make out how she felt about the business. Since hearing of the Wilson Island campaign she had seemed irritated with him — yet anxious to correct Ann's manners.

Ann suddenly laughed and then held out her hand. The young fellow bent down, took her hand in one of his and kissed it. Then Ann came trotting towards the schooner, leaving the young man looking after her dazedly.

Ann was about to come swinging up over the rail with her usual nimble grace, but she changed her mind and walked daintily along to the plank and up it with her hands splayed out to the sides as though she were terrified of losing her balance. The fellow came edging nearer, but though Ann waited for some little while balancing precariously atop the *Harraseeket*'s rail, the fellow didn't try to come up and rescue her. This, Leland thought, was to be expected of a rusticator. But that was all right — a rusticator being good for nothing as a man, it wasn't hurting anything too much to saddle one with a wife. And Ann and her mother would be all right because as long as they had the rusticator's money they could look after themselves and do what they wanted, and without even having to worry about the fellow trying to take charge.

Ann finally came on down to the deck without any help, and when she turned to wave to the fellow he seemed more assured and waved back. She laughed and went tripping along aft and below.

Hattie followed without a word, and Leland watched the young man nod at him and then turn and go slowly off.

Then Leland went below to find out all about it.

Ann was too excited to sit down. She wandered around the cabin this way and that, her eyes bright and her cheeks flushed, breaking out in merry excited laughter every few sentences. Her mother listened with a kind of bittersweet smile, hands clasped in her lap and her eyes not always seeming to focus on her daughter. Leland slipped in quietly and leaned against the bulkhead just inside the companionway.

". . . and the Lincolns have a phonograph! You put these round things in and wind it up and it plays music and people talking! I saw one in a window in Boston, but I didn't know what it was or that regular people could have them. Oh, it was so much fun! And some other people invited me to go swimming with them tomorrow if it's a nice day but I didn't say if I would or if I wouldn't!" She looked gaily at Leland and broke out in merry laughter. "I don't have a bathing dress so I guess I'll have to say no, but it would be so much fun! You know, these people are really very nice, not like Captain Wells always tells about them, just rich and stupid and useless. I could just stay here all summer with them and go walking and swimming and picnicking. Did I tell you about the picnic I was invited to for dinner? We went all the way to the other end of the island, and there's a nice little rocky point and an eagle's nest and we ate and *ate!* It was so *good!*"

She talked on in the same way for some time more about what the cottages were like, and how sometimes it was hard to think that these were really rich people because the insides of the cottages were so plain and simple and they just seemed to drop bathing suits anywhere on the floor and had hammocks on their front porches and the furniture was so old and worn and they didn't seem to worry about it very much — although they said the Farrels, whose three sons were building the cottages, *were* particular about the furniture — so Leland ought to be careful about the stuff he was unloading! But you could tell the rest were rich people too because they were so *elegant.* She paused self-consciously after using this word. Their clothes were so fine, she went on, and these people just had such an elegant *way* about them.

Finally she paused for breath and took a turn or two up and down without saying anything. Hattie leaned forward and said,

"Well, you've had quite a day, haven't you, dear? Who was the young man who walked you back?"

With a slight deepening of her blush, she said carelessly, "That was just Percy Lincoln. I think he likes me."

"Well, and do you like him?" Hattie asked smilingly.

"Oh, he's all right, I guess." She gave Leland a quick glance. He felt irritated with her. Was she playing games, or was she serious?

The next morning, Ann went again to spend the day with her friends on Wilson Island. Percy Lincoln came down to await her coming ashore, but he didn't come too near the schooner. Leland kept an eye on him as he worked away at some repairs to the *Harraseeket* — unloading had gone fast, and they had finished the previous day. Leland's opinion of the boy was low and getting lower all the time. He muttered to himself about the sissy, useless nature of the fellow and found fault with everything from how he dressed to how he stood waiting for Ann. Then Leland came around to the thought that the boy was so worthless as to be not worth wasting effort thinking about. He reminded himself that as far as he was concerned the only requirements the boy must fulfill were that he marry Ann and be able to support her and her mother. And his being on Wilson Island was proof enough of having money.

Ann, evidently following Leland's advice about how to be an attractive woman, kept Percy waiting for more than half an hour, even though she had been dressed and ready to go at breakfast, two hours before the boy's arrival at the dock. At last she appeared and waved gaily to Percy, who waved back and took a few steps towards the schooner. She swept up the deck and over the rail on the two planks laid out for the purpose, and then went running lightly up the dock to Percy, and they went on up the bank together.

While Leland took time to do a whole array of minor repairs, Ann spent three more days in more or less the same way she had the first, coming back bright-eyed and happy each time, Percy waiting for her in the mornings and walking her as far as the dock in the evenings. On the fourth evening she managed to coax him over the planks onto the deck and she rewarded him by allowing him to give her a light kiss on the cheek. Leland's jaw set hard at the sight of this kissing, and stayed that way for some time after. He did not go aft to hear the tale of the day.

Lying in his bunk in the dark forecastle that night, he tried to think rationally about the business: Things were actually going quite well — his burden might be getting closer to being lifted. But it was not until he got his mind back onto the list of things still to be done on the *Harraseeket*, and got involved in planning the details of how he would go about these repairs, that sufficient peace overtook him to allow sleep.

Three more days went by. Percy came aboard every evening and was each time rewarded by a kiss. The third night he was getting pretty cocky and went over the rail onto the dock with the air of having done so every day of his life. When Ann went aft, Leland followed her below.

"So what does this fellow say to you?" he asked her.

"And why should you care what Percy says to me?" she returned with a mischievous gleam in her eye.

She had never spoken to Leland in quite this way before, and he was taken aback for a few moments. Then he said, "Tomorrow I'm leaving here. Are you going to stay or what?"

She leaned back in her chair, lightly feeling the placement of her hair with both hands, smiling.

"I've been invited by the Lincolns to stay as long as I like," she said. "I think it would be fun." She leaned forward to put her elbows on the galley table and her chin in her hands. "I think Percy might want to marry me," she said.

"He said that?" Leland asked sharply, while Hattie said apprehensively, "But you hardly know him!"

Ann giggled. "He's so funny," she said. "He talks and talks about how pretty I am and how he can't stand being away from me for a minute and how he can't sleep for thinking about me. But I think he's afraid to ask me. I think I must be very scary to men, all dressed up!" She seemed unsure whether to be pleased or upset, and she glanced at Leland, who was frowning.

"Well, of course, you must bring him on board so we can meet him," Hattie said. One of her hands rubbed the back of the other, which was pressed down into her lap.

Ann brightened. "You know, that is just what I was going to ask. Could we take him for a little sail in the bay? It would be so much fun."

"Fun, is it," Leland muttered, preoccupied. His feelings about all that had been happening were so full of conflict he wasn't sure what he felt. What he wanted was for something to *happen*, to get the thing over with. He had the feeling Ann was playing some sort of game and he wanted to make her decide what she wanted to do and do it and quit fooling around.

"All right," he said. "But mind you make good use of it."

Ann laughed. "Can we do it tomorrow?"

"Rain or shine," he said shortly, and went out on deck.

The next day started out hot and muggy, more of what they'd been having. The breeze was very light. Ann beckoned Percy aboard and he came, and she explained that he was invited sailing. He looked apprehensive but bravely stated that that sounded like a great idea.

"This is Captain Wells," Ann said. "And my mother. This is Percy Lincoln."

Percy looked startled at Hattie being referred to as her mother, but he was polite. "Hello," he said. "Nice to meet you. What a hot day!" And he bowed to her. "Captain Wells?" he said, and held out his hand. Leland, sizing him up, took the hand and gripped it hard. Percy's eyes got big, but to his credit he didn't let on otherwise.

While Ann stood with Percy to one side, Leland prepared to get under way. She had a mischievous look on her face that Leland didn't care for.

Once they were away from the dock and gliding slowly out of Jettison Cove, Ann went below with Hattie, and Percy came back to stand near Leland.

"Have you been a seaman for a long time, Captain?" he asked in a thinnish nasal voice. Possibly it was the effort to hide his lack of ease that gave his tone a condescending air.

"A while," Leland said.

"You're from Boston then?"

"No."

"Oh." Percy looked puzzled. "Your wife is then?"

"I don't have no wife."

"Really." He looked very embarrassed. "I thought . . . you see . . . well, I naturally assumed you were her father."

"If you're wantin' my permission, you got it. Just waste no time, is my advice."

"Oh, right." Percy backed away, then acted as though he hadn't a thought on his mind and sauntered to the rail. But he was uncertain on his feet with the *Harraseeket* rolling slightly under him.

Leland thought: It must be an awful thing to grow up a rusticator and know nothing and be nothing, even if you were rich.

In a little while, Ann and Hattie appeared on deck carrying a tray of cookies and some lemonade. The sun baked down and the wind had died, and the *Harraseeket* lay rolling idly in the long low swell. While they ate cookies and drank lemonade, Hattie asked Percy all about his family. He had three brothers and a sister, all married, two of the three brothers working in the family business in New York. That business was grain — wheat, barley, and oats. His father had started the business and it was big and successful now, and once he finished school Percy expected to go into the family business too. And how did he do at school — college, was it? Yes, Harvard, and he was in his second year there. When pressed, he admitted he was not quite as brilliant as his brothers and had had some trouble staying in school.

They finished the cookies and lemonade. Leland had his eye on the thunderheads piling up to the west. You could hear rumblings now and then. But they lay becalmed.

Ann and Percy went forward and leaned over the rail to look down into the water and talk, Ann giving out a giggle every once in a while.

"Well," Hattie said to Leland, "he seems a nice boy, I suppose. Our young lady has made quite an impression. Do you think he'll really want to marry her?"

"I don't know what's holding him up, only he don't seem to carry much sail. But there ain't much to do but wait."

Hattie drew herself up. She said, "You really want to get rid of me that bad that you'd let Ann marry a worthless boy like Percy?"

"I'll bet he's worth a few dollars more than me," he said. "Ain't it unnatural quiet and hot out here though. I don't like the look of them thunderheads."

He went forward and dropped the main and foresail and pulled down the headsails as well.

"Better get below if you don't want to get wet," he said to Ann and Percy as he stepped by them.

No sooner had everyone gotten below and Leland gone back on deck in oilskins than the squall hit. The rain was blinding and the wind blew gale force. Then after only a few minutes it stopped. The rain quit and the sun showed the deck and all the rigging glistening with droplets. Two weaker squalls followed, leaving the air cooled and freshened. After a bit the wind started to blow strongly out of the northwest, kicking up whitecaps. Ann came eagerly on deck,

Percy, pale and cautious, behind her. Canvas was booming: Leland was hauling up the sails. He made it look easy, but getting sails on a schooner the size of the *Harraseeket* hauled up and set properly in a breeze of wind without the aid of a donkey engine would normally have been a two- or three-man job.

In a short time, they were close-hauled on the starboard tack, headed towards Vinalhaven. The *Harraseeket* heeled to the breeze and fairly danced over the bright lively water. For a few moments Ann stood transfixed watching the schooner sail. There was a happy, self-forgetful light in her eyes which made Leland suddenly feel close to her. Then he realized how long it had been since he'd felt comfortable around her, and with this came something much like homesickness.

But now she became aware of herself again, and she turned to Percy with that excited, mischievous look she'd been so given to recently. The change made Leland irritable.

"Kiss me!" she said to Percy.

Percy first looked startled. Then it appeared to dawn on him what she was asking, and he smiled and stepped nearer to her — but she stepped back.

"*Kiss* me," she said tauntingly, and giggled. Disconcerted, Percy stepped again towards her. The movement of the vessel under his feet made this somewhat tricky for him, but again she stepped back.

"Oh, come on," she teased him, and then she turned and went trotting lightly forward along the weather side of the deck, as though the tipped and rolling deck of the *Harraseeket* were as flat and steady as a floor. Percy paused for a moment, made his decision, and rushed forward, swaying and banging into things, clutching the rail to keep from falling. He followed Ann, who kept a taunting distance ahead of him, all the way up to the bow and then back along the lee side, over which he cast wary looks at the foaming water racing by.

From the helm, Leland watched grimly, his jaw set. Didn't the girl know better than this? Hadn't he told her plainly how she should behave? Oh yes, she knew, all right — she was doing this out of pure perversity. The stupid girl. Didn't she know she was apt to lose the fellow this way? What was the matter with her, didn't she want to get married? She ought to know Percy would be an easy husband to twist around and make sail whatever course she liked. Didn't she know that was why he'd brought her here to find a rusticator? Didn't the fool girl even know a good thing when she saw it?

Ann waited next to the main rigging until the pale-faced Percy was nearly upon her, and then suddenly, regardless of her dress, she sprang into the rigging and went aloft.

It was a moment before Percy even realized where she'd gone, and then he looked around helplessly for another moment or two. He was plainly terrified, but seeing her up there apparently resolved him and he awkwardly got himself up into the rigging and clung to it, peering terrorized at the water racing by below. Then he looked up again at Ann, who was at the crosstrees laughing down at him and encouraging him to come on up and enjoy the view with her. Determinedly he tried to climb up.

But the motion of the *Harraseeket* was more than he could manage, and when he tried to put his foot on a ratline he misjudged and his foot went beyond it instead, and in trying to push up with the other foot *it* slipped, and a jolt of the schooner shook his hands loose and there he was, hanging upside down. He may have fainted, because then his leg slipped out from between the ratlines and he fell headfirst into the water, losing his straw hat.

Leland rounded up and went back, and Ann pulled Percy out herself. He shivered and dripped, and Hattie wrapped him in a wool blanket and took him below to the galley fire.

12

Percy Lincoln, looking rather seedy, was helped up over the rail and down onto the dock by Ann. There he took his leave of her in perfunctory fashion. Ann came back aboard repentant.

"Poor Percy," she said. "I think his pride is hurt. But I didn't really mean for him to fall in the water!"

Leland ignored her as he went about some chores. He was disgusted with her. Hattie saw Percy out of sight up the hill into the woods.

"Ann dear," she said fussily, "you have nearly ruined that dress. Just look at it! And after Leland was so generous in giving you money to buy it!" She was fingering it, trying to see how much of the dirt would dust off. "And look here, it's torn!"

"I'm sorry, Mother," Ann said contritely. "Captain Wells?" She went towards him with one hand holding the other to her breast.

He didn't look around. His jaw muscles were bulging at the backs of his cheeks, his eyes blazing. He was scraping a particularly dark piece of foredeck which, under all the hot sun they'd been having lately, was showing signs of drawing open. The scraper brought up fine curls of white pine and revealed bright new yellow wood. He was on his knees to do this job, not having bothered to go hunt up the big deck scraper. Ann came and knelt near him.

"I'm sorry," she said. "I really am."

He said nothing, went on scraping.

"It's just that I couldn't resist. I just couldn't. Percy really is a nice man, you know. But how can I *respect* him? It's not his fault, and he really tries, but he is *such* a sissy. He washes his hands every minute and he is so particular about everything it about drives me crazy. Do you think he'll come back? I don't know what to say to him if he does! I really don't know what I'm doing anymore. I guess you would say that's just like a woman. That's what you would say, isn't it?" She waited, watching him work, fascinated by the sure movements of his hands and anxious for a reply. "Leland?" she said, in a small voice.

Leland swallowed.

"I think the best thing would be just to leave," she said finally, slumping. "I don't have to take a long time to make up my mind. I would never marry Percy Lincoln."

"All right," he said wearily, and got up, barely glancing at her, to set about getting under way.

Leland didn't have a freight lined up and so sailed for Frenchman Bay hoping to find one. The northwesterly held, blowing hard, and they made Frenchman Bay in fairly short order. But to get up the bay they had to haul up hard on the wind and beat in, and it was a slow business.

Ann changed out of her damaged dress into her deckhand's clothes and helped tack the schooner. She did her best to be what she used to be before she'd ever put on a dress, but Leland wasn't reassured. As far as he was concerned, her antics with the rusticator made her motives forever suspect, and he was determined not to be influenced by her any further. That evening they made Flanders Bay. After supper when Leland went on deck to give it the nightly wash-down, Ann came out to help him.

"You know, I really am sorry," she said. "I don't know why I did that. But I promise I won't do it again. It was such a stupid thing to do. Will you forgive me?"

"It's all right," he said. "You're only a woman and don't know no better."

"But I don't *want* to be a woman — I want to be your friend. I want to be . . . oh, I don't know."

She stood helplessly, an empty canvas bucket in her hands, looking at him pleadingly. He felt an urge to go and comfort her or help her somehow, but used all his willpower to resist it — that way lay great danger, he knew instinctively.

"I don't know what I can tell you," he said carefully. "You have to figure out what you think yourself."

"Do you love me?" she asked him.

Leland's breath caught and he fairly prickled all over with sudden fear. It took a few moments for him to get hold of himself. When he thought he had, he said, "You've got to get them kinds of ideas out of your head. I told you before, I ain't wanting a wife."

"But why not?"

"Just put them ideas out of your head, that's all." He walked away from her. She looked after him thoughtfully and then went below.

Later that evening Leland saw that Ann had put on a clean dress and, with her mother's help, was working at cleaning and repairing the damaged one. A great deal of confiding seemed to be going on between them, and they appeared to be on the best terms, with a sense of newly discovered common ground that brought them closer than they had probably ever been before.

I don't want anything to do with that, he thought to himself as he went forward to the forecastle. Nothing to do with that at all.

The northwesterly blew all night, didn't quit until just before dawn, and in the morning when Leland went on deck for a look at the weather there was a strange schooner anchored not fifty yards away. She was a handsome little vessel just about the same size as the *Harraseeket*, carrying two topmasts and power in the yawl-boat, the latter of which was not yet that common in small coasters. Leland, like most coastermen in those days, knew every schooner that regularly worked where he did, but he had never seen this one before. He gave her a good looking over and then was about to start aft when two men appeared on the other schooner's deck.

"It's Frank!" Ann said. She was sitting on the *Harraseeket*'s main hatch combing her hair, her dress flowing around her, and Leland hadn't even been aware she was on deck until she spoke. "And Captain Smith," she added in a subdued tone.

That was who they were, all right. They stood on the deck of the other schooner and stared at Ann. Suddenly, Myatt Smith strode aft to ready his yawl-boat, Frank lending a hand and finally coming along with evident reluctance.

Leland stood watching with his hands on his hips, glaring across at Myatt. The first sight of the man had made anger rise in him, and it was still rising.

"Go below," he barked at Ann. She was on her feet now, and just stared at the oncoming yawl-boat. She didn't seem to be aware of Leland at all. He said, "Go *below*, do you hear me?"

She looked around at him for a moment, but it was evident her thoughts were elsewhere and she still hadn't understood what he had said. Leland was furious. He strode to her. But his wariness of her femininity, together with an awareness that she was not deliberately defying him but only distracted, made him gentle as he took hold of her shoulders and turned her aft and gave her a push. She stumbled a few steps in that direction, but then she looked again at the yawl-boat now arriving alongside, and straight into Myatt's frank stare. She was still there when Myatt swung aboard and took three long steps to reach her. She tried to meet his gaze but ended up looking down at his huge boots.

Myatt reached out a hand as if he had thought to lift her chin, but hesitated and drew his hand back.

"Hello," he said, his voice awkwardly youthful and respectful. "I'm Myatt Smith. Who're you?"

"Ann Procter," she said in a voice barely audible.

"Ann Procter . . . *Ann Procter?*"

"Yes," she said, and looked up at him, blushing overwhelmingly but also smiling a very feminine smile of pleasure at her effect on him.

"What do you want?" Leland said to Myatt, coming near and giving him his most withering glare.

"Why, I just came to pay a social call," Myatt said, recovering himself to some degree.

"You go on below and help your mother," Leland said to Ann. "Go on."

She looked up at Myatt and smiled and then went off with erect grace. Both men watched her go, neither moving a muscle. She smiled and waved to them both just before disappearing down the companionway.

Myatt vented a great sigh. Then he turned and held out his hand to Leland, beaming.

"Well, how are ye, Leland?" he said broadly.

Leland did not take the hand. "Now you listen to me, Myatt," he said. "I want you to keep your hands off that girl. You understand me? She ain't one of your kind and I ain't having you runnin' afoul of her."

Myatt's brow darkened. "Well, that's a right friendly piece of advice you be handing to me. Like as not it's given out free, and that's a good thing because I'd be madder'n tunket if I had to pay for it."

"Well, if you don't take it, I'll see you *do* pay for it, and it won't be a price cal'lated to dreen your wallet neither."

Myatt was swelling himself up to make an answer to this when Ann appeared aft.

"Captain Smith!" she called in her gayest manner. "Won't you stay to breakfast? And Frank, too. Where is he? Didn't he come aboard?"

Frank was still in the yawl-boat alongside. He came over the rail, after direct invitation from Ann, wary and sheepish. They all went below to breakfast, Myatt beaming broadly again.

It turned out that the ship Myatt had been master of had been sold and laid up in New York without ever sailing for Rio. Myatt had been discharged as captain and there being nothing better in the offing he had taken over as master of the schooner *J W Hanson*. "Just for a little change," he boomed out jovially with a broad, offhand, easy laugh. Frank had needed a berth and Myatt needed a good hand who knew the coasting trade, so here they were, calculating to load some lumber or shooks or anything else that came to hand — the owners weren't particular, just so the schooner paid good dividends.

Myatt was animated and his eyes and teeth gleamed within the wreath of his black beard. "You know how owners are," he boomed with boisterous good nature, "they don't care if a vessel is fit only for the ship-breakers or if the crew gets drownded — just so she pays dividends regular!"

"Your schooner looks quite new and well-found," Hattie said. She had looked put out when she saw Myatt, and her brow furrowed when her eye fell on Ann's smiles and bright eyes.

"Oh, the *Hanson* ain't really so bad," Myatt admitted. "But that's because I didn't take the first schooner I come acrost, but picked her out as one that might not sink under me the first good blow. But her being a mostly sound boat ain't no fault of the owners, I can tell you!"

Ann laughed openmouthed and wide-eyed, watching Myatt's every gesture with newfound boldness and pleasure.

Leland ate nothing and simply glared at Myatt in open hatred. Frank sat back from the table after eating a little and watched the proceedings apprehensively. Myatt paid attention to none of them but Ann.

After some time, Myatt seemed to run out of anecdotes and entertaining commentary on things in general. He pushed back from the table, put a big hand on a big knee in preparation for getting to his feet, and said, "Where be ye bound then? Any freights to be had in these parts?"

"Oh, Leland says there ought to be something here somewhere," Ann said, "but he hasn't found one yet."

"Well, I guess somethin'll turn up," Myatt said, and got up. Leland, who had never left off his cold stare, followed Myatt closely to the rail. Ann smiled up at Myatt as he turned to say goodby to her.

"You'll have to visit again," she said hopefully. "You will, won't you?"

"Just see if you can keep me away!" he said, and gave Leland a quick sidelong glance.

Myatt and Frank were no sooner over the side and cast off than Leland went forward and started heaving short his anchor. Ann sauntered around stretching her legs and arms and smiling into the sky.

"Isn't he a nice man?" she said exultantly.

"You don't want to get mixed up with him," Leland told her tersely. "You'll be sorry."

"How could I be sorry?" she asked, seeming surprised.

"You don't know him, and I do. You stay away from him."

She giggled. "I think you're just jealous," she said and went capering off down the deck.

"Damn-fool girl," he muttered.

<hr />

13

The northwesterly having blown itself out, there was a near-calm, with light and fitful breezes from here and then there. Leland sent the *Harraseeket* drifting west across Frenchman Bay. He thought that when the tide started to come in it might bring the southerly with it, and he hoped to tide up the Skillings River with a fair wind. Leland had a nose for finding business and often he would take a notion and pick an obscure cove or inlet apparently at random, and there somebody would be with a load of something ready to go. Leland's choice of the Skillings River was partly a result of following his nose and partly just an urge to sail into a place he hadn't been in some time.

Behind him less than a hundred yards off was the *J W Hanson*. When the wind finally did begin to freshen a little from the south, both schooners were getting near the mouth of the river, and when Leland bore off to sail up the river so did the *Hanson*. Leland swore and jibed over all standing and hauled onto the wind. The *Hanson* did the same. Leland swore again.

Ann, who had been below, came on deck, sweeping by Leland at the wheel in a manner calculated to catch his eye. She went forward to sit on the hatch. She let down her hair again and brushed it, shaking it out with her head tipped back.

Leland found his eyes straying to her now and then, and every time it happened he grew more annoyed with her and with himself. There was no point sailing off like this across the bay. The *Hanson* was not likely to be an easy vessel to leave behind, and in any case if the *Harraseeket* put in anywhere long enough to load there would be ample time for the *Hanson* to catch up. Yet he couldn't bring himself to turn back.

Ann got up and came aft, her hair all carefully arranged on her head with various pins. She stood close to Leland and waved a white handkerchief at the other schooner and got an enthusiastic wave in return from Myatt.

"You'll have to go back there to load sometime," she said to Leland. "And so will Myatt." She was standing very close now, so that her perfume seemed to enclose him like a small forecastle in a bad storm.

"I'll decide where I have to go," he said shortly. He felt warm and it was hard not to glance at her, especially as she was making every effort to catch his eye — but for the moment he managed it.

"Myatt will go wherever you do," she said in a most reasonable tone — but there was that mischievousness of hers behind it. "Or, I should say, he'll go wherever I am."

The worst of it was, he was sure she was quite correct.

She sauntered in front of him as though wandering aimlessly and unaware she was distracting him; then she went below again.

"All right," Leland muttered through his teeth, "you want to play that game, play it, but don't expect me to, and don't come crying to me when the line snubs short."

He sailed the *Harraseeket* around onto the other tack — the *Hanson* doing likewise — and went back to the Skillings River.

There was a pole wharf not too far up, in a little indentation in the shore, and there were a lot of staves and shooks there, bound up to the westward. Both schooners began loading almost immediately. Myatt and Frank were able to load more quickly than Leland, who had to do all his own stowing, and when they were finished Myatt insisted on helping Leland load. All this took a little more than a week, and Myatt and Ann spent every evening together, usually taking a walk and then going aboard the *Harraseeket* to play checkers. Ann was very good at checkers and she won much more often than she lost, but Myatt only seemed eager to come back for another try — to Ann's great delight and amusement. She made him the butt of all kinds of jokes about it, and he would laugh broadly and offhandedly, as though it didn't matter to him in the least, and then set to work very seriously to try to beat her.

Leland kept his mouth shut. Being helpless to prevent events, his attitude was that he had washed his hands of the matter. He stayed away from the sight of Ann and Myatt together because it made him feel like pitching Myatt overboard. And Ann sometimes seemed to want to play him off against Myatt, a game he was determined not to play. The very idea of it made him furious.

Hattie considered that he had given up the fight at the time when he should have put on a real campaign. The thing was, she didn't care for Myatt. Leland knew that more than once she had taken Ann aside and given her a lecture about not letting her head be turned by such a drunken careless man as he was. But Myatt was on his best behavior. There was never the smell of drink on his breath, he was quite considerate and polite, and he had even toned down some of his jovial joking. He seemed to have been somewhat tamed by Ann's presence, and whenever Hattie tried to lecture, Ann simply pointed out these facts and seemed to delight the more in the man's company.

But Leland knew Myatt, and it seemed to him that though for the moment the intoxicating presence of Ann might be enough for Myatt, there would come a time sooner or later when the old ways would out. It had happened before at least twice that Leland knew of, and when the effect of the woman wore off, Myatt had gone back to drink in grand style with a long binge. Leland didn't try to tell Ann this. He felt sure she'd only think he was competing for her attentions. He thought he would bide his time and let her find it out for herself.

The morning they put to sea the wind was fresh out of the south-southwest. They had the ebb tide with them but needed to tow out of the river. Leland's motor wouldn't start. He fiddled with it while Myatt came over in his yawl-boat to try to help. Leland told him to just go on ahead, he'd get her fixed up soon enough.

"Well, hell," Myatt said. "They's plenty power in my yawl-bo't. I'll just put a line on you and out we'll go."

Leland was not in a good mood for thinking about having to put up with Myatt's presence wherever he went, and Myatt's offering to tow him was like rubbing salt in the wound. He once again told Myatt to go on ahead, and again Myatt wouldn't hear of it. Ann was at the after rail of the *Harraseeket* looking down on the proceedings, and she told Leland that she thought he was being stubborn and foolish. "Here Myatt is trying to help you and all you can do is get angry at him," she said.

Leland steadfastly refused the tow and finally got his motor going, but Myatt had waited for him and Leland was in a very foul mood by the time the two schooners reached the more open waters of Frenchman Bay and began to beat for the open sea.

The *Hanson* was a fast schooner to windward in a good breeze and right off she began to pull slightly ahead. Leland let this go on without attempting to do anything about it until Myatt made a show of luffing to wait for him. Then, though the motive hardly rested on reason, Leland put a becket on the wheel and went aloft and cast the gaskets off the main topsail. The *Harraseeket* held a course so well with a becket on the wheel that she was still driving to windward full and by, and Leland went hand over hand across the spring stay to the foremast and cast the gaskets off the fore-topsail as well before coming down to the deck and hauling these sails up, sheeting them down and heaving down their tacks. He made it all look easy and did it with amazing speed. When he returned to the helm, Hattie was standing on deck watching him with her hands on her hips and the first smile she'd had for him in more than two weeks. Ann was pointedly not noticing him, waving her handkerchief at Myatt in the *Hanson*, which now lay a short distance under their lee and just aft — so confident was Myatt in the superiority of his schooner. Myatt had sent Frank aloft to shake out the *Hanson*'s topsails, however.

Leland remembered a flying jib he had in the sail locker and again dropped a becket casually over a spoke on the wheel and went forward to break out this new sail. He set it and then went back to the wheel, tossed off the becket, planted his feet, and began nursing the *Harraseeket* over every wave.

But the *Hanson* set a sail to match, and the result was she held her place — except that she seemed to sail very slightly nearer the wind. They went charging across the upper waters of the bay and then tacked. And here was where Leland was handicapped. He had to go aloft and pass the fore-topsail over the spring stay and reset it in order to come about. This took time and after one tack the *Hanson* was ahead and no longer to leeward, having drawn even. By the time they got by the Porcupine Islands, Myatt was handily ahead mostly because of this complication in tacking. In the *Hanson*, Frank went aloft to pass the fore-topsail while Myatt charged all over the deck doing a single-handed boxhaul, which speeded up tacking still more. Leland had to set the wheel for a slow sail around while he went aloft to pass the topsail.

By the time they had made the open sea Myatt was well ahead and to windward. It was pretty well a dead muzzler out in the open and breezing on enough that neither schooner really should have been carrying topsails, but neither captain was going to be the first to take them in, so they stayed up.

Off and on the coast they lay. Now the tacks were long, and despite having to go aloft and shift the fore-topsail over, Leland caught up, and for a while it was so even that when they crossed tacks sometimes one and sometimes the other vessel had to drop to leeward and let the other pass. Then Leland clearly began to lead: he knew how to get the best advantage out of the slants of wind in under the land. But after three tacks which ever more dramatically proved the lead, Myatt made a very long tack seaward looking for more wind yet than they already had, going hull down over the horizon. Leland stayed nearer the shore and continued to play the deflections under the land to advantage. But when Myatt came back from seaward he was ahead by perhaps fifty yards, and Ann cheered and waved. Myatt grinned and waved back while Leland stonily ignored the other schooner.

Myatt went far to sea again, and Leland again used all his considerable skill to play the slants of wind under the land to advantage, but now when Myatt returned from seaward he was well over a hundred yards ahead. Again Ann cheered and waved and again Myatt waved back.

Myatt never lost his advantage the rest of the day. Leland stubbornly kept trying to get advantage from the wind under the shore and Myatt kept making long tacks offshore, and the results remained ever the same. Leland would have sailed past the cove Myatt anchored in if the wind had held, but it died out and long after Myatt and Frank had gasketed topsails, lowered away and stoppered the foresail, put a watch tackle on the main, furled the jibs, sluiced the decks, and gone below, the *Harraseeket* finally came crawling to anchor nearby. Leland hated anchoring in the same cove, but his pride would not let him anchor anywhere short, and it was no good towing beyond — Myatt would simply follow. Myatt came over in his yawl-boat as soon as they arrived.

As he swung over the fly rail aft and swaggered across the deck holding out his big hand to Leland, grinning, Leland just watched him balefully.

"I was afraid you 'uz never going to show up," Myatt said. "I be very glad ye did though!" He beamed down at Ann, who had spent considerable time on her toilet as the day drew towards its close. Myatt was himself freshly bathed and in his best clothes. "Aren't you going to congratulate Myatt?" Ann said to Leland as he turned away. "I bet he would have congratulated you!"

Leland glanced her up and down disgustedly and turned away again to go forward.

"Don't mind him," Myatt said to Ann. "He ain't used to it, I reckon. I never heard tell of anybody beating him to windward in a schooner anywhere near the size of the *Harraseeket*. And he didn't have no crew, you got to remember. He done pretty good sailing with topsails all alone. Say, you want to play checkers? I'm just a-hankering to play you while I got the better of the Good Lord and the ebb tide."

"Are you sure?" Ann teased him. "That sounds to me like a sore temptation to Providence."

Weeks, then months went by; the summer passed into autumn. Myatt saw to it that he was seldom away from the *Harraseeket* for very long, though there were a couple of periods of over a week when he and his schooner were elsewhere — during which times he might have done some drinking, Leland suspected. Whenever they did see him he appeared sober and easygoing. But Leland was confidently waiting for the day Ann's influence on Myatt wore off sufficiently that the man reverted to his old ways.

Yet, by the time the leaves started to turn golden and red and it was pretty plain which way things were headed between Ann and Myatt, there was still no sign of reversion. It became a worrisome question whether Myatt would remain convincingly reformed until after the wedding.

One cool October evening when the schooners were anchored not far from each other in a cove along the Mussel Ridge Channel and there was enough nip in the air that it felt like frost, Ann was aboard the *Hanson* and Leland and Hattie were eating supper alone with the galley stove radiating welcome warmth. By this time Leland was well used to Hattie's presence and never thought twice about her doing all the cooking, washing up, and cleaning of clothes. He and Hattie even seemed able to respect each other's territory and get along after a fashion — not that his opinion of her was much higher now than before. But he had long since decided it did no good to make an issue of it all the time. He refrained from showing his opinions of her and of her presence on board and she refrained from provoking him on most occasions.

But tonight certain feelings of hers could be held in no longer, and she allowed the silence to draw on only a few minutes before she said, "If you don't do something, they're going to get married, you know."

"I've said what I've had to say to her. I can't help it if she won't listen. If she wants to marry him, that's her affair."

"But she's still only a foolish girl. I don't think she knows the kind of man Myatt really is."

"I know she don't. But I can't help it if she's determined to find out about him the hard way."

Hattie's brows furrowed. She had been looking more careworn lately.

"I think you could still have her," she said. "But you have to let her know you want her. You can't just give up every time Myatt seems to win out. I have talked to Frank about Myatt, and he has told me some things about Myatt's drinking and the kinds of things he has done, and I've tried to tell her, but she won't listen to me. I'm only her mother and I don't know anything. But I know she still cares for you. She'll *listen* to you . . . "

"No she won't. I told her way back to stay away from Myatt, but that didn't turn out any great kill-or-cure. She just wants to play games."

"But don't you see? You've abandoned her — you haven't made any claim to her. You know you should, Leland."

Leland started to reply, but changed his mind and studied his chowder.

"The silly girl thinks that just because Myatt is a deepwater captain and has been everywhere and can beat you in a schooner race he is a better man than you are. And she thinks she has him all tamed because she can beat him at checkers, but you don't tame a man like Myatt. But he takes her around to all the socializing he can find to go to and you don't, so she thinks he's more her type than you are. You ought to take her a few places yourself, and maybe that would wake her up. I'll bet if you kissed her once she would change a few of her ideas about you in a hurry! She's only a young girl and she doesn't know what she wants, and she has a big idea of her effect on Myatt. You could make her see the truth. But you have to let her know you *want* her — and don't try to pretend to me that you *don't* want her, I can see it in your eyes every time you look at her. And you have said yourself that she has more sense than most girls and is more useful. I know I was never very useful to Dan as a schooner-man's wife. He didn't mind, but I could have been much more help to him than I was. But Ann is different. Of course, once she has some children to look after you'll have to make allowances. But she is just the right one for you, it is so plain to me."

Leland's existence had been reasonably well-ordered recently and his thoughts had been strictly under control, but Hattie's talk brought all kinds of unruly desires, fears, hopes, and confusions back into plain view. This made it impossible to think how to answer her, and not being firmly in control made him angry. He just glared back at her. But she actually smiled at him.

"You know," she went on, "you and I never got along very well, and that was quite a lot my fault. I have to say I was wrong about you. Being here on the *Harraseeket* all summer I have found out that you aren't the kind of man I thought you were. You really are a sober, hard-working, good man. You have some very backward opinions and you are awful stubborn and bullheaded, but if Ann married you my heart would be at rest about her and I would be so proud. I know you both would be happy. But please listen to me this time, Leland. You have to *do* something, or she will marry that man. I know she will."

Leland never answered her a word. He glared around but couldn't even begin to think what to say. As soon as he was finished eating he went on deck. He recalled dimly that there were some frayed servings aloft that he had been meaning to renew, and he got what he needed for the job and climbed aloft.

Once at the crosstrees he settled himself and set to work. Gradually the confusion and terrors were forgotten, displaced by the familiar motions of laying on the turns of the new serving. Before long he was quite content and totally unaware of the existence of Hattie and Ann and Myatt. By the time the gathering darkness sent him back down he was in a good mood, a sense of peace and well-being having settled over him. He went straight below to his bunk in the forecastle and turned in with his head full of possible plans for the morrow, depending on what the weather did.

But sometime in the night he awoke frightened, short of breath. Suppose Ann actually married Myatt, without knowing what he was going to one day be like? What might happen to her? Yet, what could he do about it? Short of trying to convince her to marry him instead, nothing. *Damn* the fool girl.

Frank had been keeping to himself for the most part, so when he announced that he was getting married to Susanna in a few days' time, everybody was put in a flutter of surprise. The schooners were in Portland, Leland there to take a freight of grain bound up Bangor River, and Myatt following suit for the obvious reason. But once Frank made his sudden announcement neither Hattie nor Ann would hear of leaving until after the wedding, though both schooners were loaded. Myatt was willing enough to stay and the three of them spent much time up in town, with Frank and Susanna and various of Susanna's relatives, buying clothes and making preparations. Frank asked Leland if he would be his best man, but Leland would have nothing whatsoever to do with the business; so Myatt took on that responsibility with pleasure. Leland mostly remained aboard the *Harraseeket* catching up on minor repairs, but he went ashore a few times looking for deals on pine tar, oakum, line, and so forth.

On the night two days ahead of Frank's wedding, Leland was sitting alone in his forecastle looking over a tub of line he'd bought cheaply at an auction the day before. There was a light tap on the companionway.

"Come in," he said, without looking up.

"Are you very busy?" Ann asked.

"I'd thought you'd be off with Smith," he said. "Where is he then?"

"I told him I had a headache."

"And do you?"

"No. May I sit down?"

"All right." He remained seated on his apple crate with his feet out in front of him and rope across his lap from a tub on one side to another tub on the other. She sat down and smoothed her dress. It was a white dress and looked to him to be the same she wore the first time he had seen her wearing one — if it wasn't he couldn't tell the difference.

"Are you going to Frank's wedding?" she asked him.

"And why should I do that?"

"How can you talk that way? And Frank your friend! Don't you know what it would mean to him to have you come?"

"It don't mean nothing to him," Leland said shortly. "Anyway, if he wants to make the biggest mistake of his life, that's his affair. It ain't none of mine."

"But that's an awful thing to say! Susanna is really a very nice person, I think. But if you won't do it for him, will you do it for me?"

Leland didn't answer right away, mechanically pulling the line through his hands, twisting it to open the lay now and then, flexing it. He was struggling with his irritation at Ann for acting about as womanlike as it was possible to act, trying to make him do something for no other reason than because she wanted him to.

"It ain't your affair either," he said measuredly. "There's no reason why you should care whether I go to Frank's wedding or not."

"But I *do* care! All right, you want to know why? Because I know Frank would like it so much."

"Why is it that women are always taking up for somebody else when it ain't none of their business?"

Ann's hands tremblingly smoothed her dress. "You can be so *heartless* sometimes, Leland Wells," she said.

He said nothing.

She got up.

"You know, I would have been so proud to sit there with you at Frank's wedding," she said. "But you don't *care*." And she started angrily for the companionway, Leland staring after her.

Then she turned back on him. "Myatt wants me to marry him," she said. "And I'm going to say yes!" Her voice went up wildly as she finished this speech. She whirled around and groped for the companionway, started up the steps.

Leland came to his feet. In a bellowing roar of a voice that shook the deck under their feet, he said, "*You get back here and sit down!*"

She turned to look at him, her face white and startled, her hands reaching behind her for something to fall back against. His eyes blazed. After a moment she came timidly back and sat down, peering up at him in a fright.

His reaction had surprised him as much as it had her, and he hadn't any idea what to do next. He stepped around behind her to get away from her gaze and gain time to recover his wits. All he was aware of was that he was furious and that he intended to do something.

He looked down at her narrow shoulders, the wispy hairs at her neck, the full gentle curves of her breasts, her small hands gripping each other in her lap. The urge to put his hands on her shoulders was so overwhelming that he nearly lost his balance, and he had to close his eyes and hold his breath and concentrate to regain control of himself.

He turned half away and looked into the darkness of an after corner of the forecastle. For years after, whenever he looked into that corner he remembered the peculiar atmosphere of this moment.

"You don't know Myatt," he said hoarsely, in a low voice. "He drinks a lot of rum. He likes to gamble. He has spent a lot of time at places like Clara's where Susanna used to be. Some of his tales about what he has done — well, I don't expect he has told you any of them." He paused, and when he went on his voice was near cracking with the overwhelming sense of tender concern he felt. "Frank told me that when Myatt doesn't expect to see you for a few days or longer he catches up on his rum drinking, and then sobers up and makes a big point of making sure he doesn't smell of it when it comes time to see you. Please listen to me, Ann. You just don't know the kind of man Myatt is."

"Yes, I do," she said. "I know all about that. He told me about it himself. But he's doing much better now, and if he does drink some when he's away from me, it's only because he can't stand to be away. Most men do drink some liquor, you know. I'd be acting pretty high and mighty to refuse him for that. And I *love* him. He makes me feel that it's *good* to be a woman. I know who I am when I'm around him."

"You think you've got him all tamed down, but you just don't know him. I know of two other girls who thought they had tamed him, too, but it wore off. One of them he dumped ashore someplace in Brazil, and the other he left on the dock at Baltimore looking pretty bruised up. There, those are awful things to have to tell you, but I'd hate for you to find it out after it was too late."

Ann stood, turning to confront him. Her eyes had a deadly glint. "Is this all you have to say to me?" she asked in a tightly controlled voice.

He looked her straight in the eye, fiercely, but he felt undercut by a sense of how futile his efforts were. She was not going to credit what he was telling her. There was nothing he could say or do. The frustration of it turned his painfully aching tenderness to rage.

"Well, if you won't hear sense, I got no more to say," he said. "Marry him and be damned."

She turned away from him and rose up the steps of the companionway with resolute dignity. His last glimpse of her left him with the impression of something glistening, but it was not until some time later that he wondered if she might have been crying.

14

By 1947 the Maine coast of 1905 was long gone. Back in 1905 there were sailing coasters to be seen everywhere. In 1947 there were only a few hulks rotting on mud flats, rigging gone or hanging in tangles, paint worn and weathered off, and decks caving in. A great deal had happened in the forty-two years from 1905 to 1947.

Shortly after marrying Ann Procter, Myatt Smith had gotten a deepwater command, and he took his wife to sea with him. After that voyage, Ann never went to sea with him again.

Frank's wife wouldn't hear of him going off for long periods and so he had taken back his old berth on the *Harraseeket*. Leland gave him mate's pay — plus a gift of one hundred dollars which he refused to admit was in any way a wedding gift. Hattie went to live in Myatt's ancestral home in Portland, so Leland and Frank were able to go back to living and working as they had before the rescue of Ann and her mother from the wreck of the *Sarah*. This lasted for a couple of years, and then Frank turned to farming, under pressure from his wife. Leland did not take on another hand, though plenty would have been willing to go in the *Harraseeket*. He worked all the time and his reputation as a sharp trader and smart-sailing master increased. He became something of a legend sailing his schooner single-handed, without even so much as a donkey engine to help. There were endless tales told about him, some with a basis in fact, but many more were pure fancy.

One favorite story was that he would never tie up at a wharf if there was a woman or a girl standing on it, and that this was why you almost never saw him going to the Maine Central wharf in Rockland, there frequently being women among those waiting for passenger steamers. Another favorite was that one winter evening he came across a schooner wrecked on an island in Penobscot Bay and saw only the captain's wife standing on the shore waving at him for help, and the first thing he did was holler to ask if the captain was still healthy. Only when she hollered back that he was fine would Leland go ashore to help them. These stories were told and retold as sober truth, despite the fact that he did still come fairly regularly to the Maine Central wharf, and despite his never having failed to lend a hand to a vessel in trouble.

In 1928 Myatt Smith died of liver troubles brought on by heavy drinking. He was forty-eight. He and Ann had had no children. Ann remained living in the same house with her mother. In 1947, Hattie died. Ann sold the house and moved to South Freeport, to a little cottage that overlooked the Harraseeket River.

This was in September. She had been there one week when she looked out her living-room window not long before sundown and saw something that made her gasp.

"Oh my heavens," she said aloud, hanging onto the back of a chair.

What she was looking at was the last holdout of the age of commercial sail in America — the *Harraseeket*, Leland Wells, master.

Ann flew out of the cottage like a girl. She was fifty-nine, but right now she looked, at any distance at all, a teen-ager. There were wrinkles in her brow and her clothes were out of fashion, but otherwise she remained a young woman, retaining her beautiful smile and her natural grace and even a good deal of her nimbleness.

She went down the steep hill and out onto the public dock. The *Harraseeket* was fifty-four years old, and she looked it even at a distance — her sails were patched and grey and she was badly hogged.

Looking weather-beaten and big in the little harbor of small pleasure and work boats, she came deliberately into the wind and dropped her anchor. Ann saw the solid, white-haired figure on deck and knew Leland immediately, though she hadn't seen him in forty-two years. She stood watching to see if he were going to come ashore, but he did not. She finally went back up to her cottage and sat looking out the window at the *Harraseeket* until the light faded. Sitting there, remembering past events, she looked more her actual age.

Early the next morning she was on the dock again. Leland appeared on deck a little later than he used to — but he was now eighty-two years old and maybe he had slowed down some.

He moved around the deck rather aimlessly for a while, and

then went below again. There was something about the way he behaved that alarmed Ann.

There was a fisherman getting ready to go out to his lobster boat in a skiff, and she asked him if he would take her out to the schooner. He said he would, but that she'd have to get herself back if she didn't want to wait until he came back that night. She said she'd manage, and the fisherman took her out. He was surprised at the practiced ease with which Ann went up over the rail.

Everything aboard the *Harraseeket* looked old and worn to a dangerous degree. The halyards were all frayed and weathered to the core. The ironwork was all rusty. The deck was worn and there were rot pockets near deckhouses and against stanchion posts. The sight of the dilapidation frightened her. She went aft and tapped on the companionway door.

Leland didn't answer the knock — was he deaf in his old age? She pushed back the slide and opened the doors and went down into the dimness below.

Leland lay on his back in his bunk, his head turned towards the door to see who was coming, but there wasn't much interest expressed in his weathered and careworn old face. His eyes didn't pierce as they used to. He squinted against the light from the open companionway.

"Leland?" she said.

His eyes widened and he looked startled. He lifted his head and blinked.

"Is that *you*, Ann?"

She came near and smiled down at him, and his eyes began to water. He swung out of the bunk and got his feet planted on the deck.

"Where'd you come from?" he asked her. Then, with sudden briskness, "Sit down, sit down. No use to stand up. Here." He held a chair for her. She gave him her dazzling smile and sat down.

They talked for hours. First Ann told him briefly what had happened to her, and then he told her some things that had happened to him, but mostly from times years ago.

"Well," she said, "and here you are still sailing. I thought there was nobody coasting anymore."

"Well, it ain't so good," he said. "Truth to tell, I ain't had a freight all this season. And I been running on savings for three years. But there ain't no more money now."

"Well, what will you do then?"

"I dunno."

"Oh, Leland," she said, and then they sat in silence for some time. There was a faint squeaking and creaking from somewhere in the *Harraseeket*.

"You'll never know how I missed this boat," she said softly. "And you. I was really such a fool to marry Myatt the way I did. I don't know why I didn't listen to you. But I thought he was capable of anything, and I knew there was no way I could ever make a fool of him. I knew he was wild and wanton, a drinker and a gambler, but I was so sure that I could change him, that all he needed was me. Oh, what vanity! My my. But what I found out was that he was really a weak man. I'll never forget the day I found out what he was like drunk. We were at sea halfway to Rio and he'd had some trouble with the crew. I guess he couldn't hold out any longer. The steward tried to protect me from him, but all he got for his trouble was a broken arm and some broken ribs. I was terrified. But there wasn't anywhere I could go. Fortunately, he didn't actually hurt me, but I nearly left him when we got back to Portland. I never went to sea with him again. I was glad when he was away, although he really did behave himself fairly well most of the time when he was home — at least I think he really tried. He'd go away for days at a time sometimes, but when he was in the house he was usually sober. I think he was always a little afraid of Mother, and that might be partly what made him behave himself when he was at home.

"But then he came home to stay because he couldn't get a ship to sail. His reputation had caught up with him for one thing; also there just weren't many deep-sea commands in square-riggers. I was scared at first, but he started to fall apart and then I began to feel sorry for him. He was not a bad man, really; he just had come to depend too much on his rum. When things went wrong, rum was the first thing he thought of to get him through his troubles. He thought of rum before he thought of me . . . the rum finally killed him. . . . I did love him though, I really did, and I wouldn't have ever left him, even though I sometimes felt like it. He really did love me, too, and he *tried* to be what I wished he was. But when he finally died I was relieved, because he was in such a mess by then. The poor man.

"But here you are, still straight and strong, and you can sit here and tell me that you haven't been able to make the *Harraseeket* pay for three years and that you haven't even had one cargo all this year and that your savings are all gone and you don't know what you'll do now — and do I find you drunk or blubbering or cursing everybody else for your troubles? No! Mother was right. I should have found some way to make you marry me! We would have been so happy. But we're old now."

"Old and useless, I guess. Ain't no more call for a schooner to haul anything anymore."

"Oh, Leland," she said feelingly, and reached across the galley table to lay a hand on one of his. He stared at it uncertainly.

"Well," he said in a way that summed up the situation and rejected sentiment as worthless.

"What will you *do?*" she asked.

"I don't *know*," he said, drawing back and giving her a look in which there was a flicker of his old piercing gaze.

"But you'll do something. You've held out longer than anybody else. I believe in you. You really *are* capable of anything."

"Well, there ain't much to believe in now," he said. "I guess me and the old *Harraseeket*'ll just have to haul up somewhere and rot away."

"You know," she said, reaching to lay a hand on one of his again, "it's as though you're married to the *Harraseeket*. You've had a long happy marriage, but she is dying and you are going to be a widower. There's nothing you can do about that. The world has left the *Harraseeket* behind. Nobody wants her for anything anymore and so her life is over."

"That's so," he said. "And I guess I ain't wanted no more either, so I'm done for, too. I never fitted nowhere else but on the *Harraseeket*."

"That's not true," she said emphatically. "You *are* wanted. *I* want you. And you used to want me, only you were already married to the *Harraseeket* so you had to choose, and you weren't going to give her up. She's a grand old lady and I can see why you love her. But you have to lay her to rest now, and there's no choice about it. But I'm still alive, and I'm long since a lonely widow, and you can have me, if you don't mind that I'm getting to be an old lady."

Leland got up and went to look out a port.

"You don't owe me anything," he said. "And you ain't so old as you seem to think. If you want to get married again, find yourself some younger fellow. You don't want an old geezer like me. I'm apt to be called aft any minute."

"I don't believe that," she said.

Leland stood for some time just looking out the port.

"She ain't far from going down," he said. "Her seams are getting mighty hollow and her bones are pretty limber. Setting here she's all right, but push her at all and I can't keep her pumped out, even with that donkey engine I finally put in."

He paused a long time. "I don't know how I'll be able to give her up though. Coastin's all I know. I couldn't live ashore, it just ain't natural-like for me. I never could feel comfortable around people ashore. Always felt crowded, and I never could figure what to say to people that wasn't worse than saying nothing at all. On my own vessel I know what I'm doing and why I'm doing it and I don't have to talk to nobody about it nor explain it nor ask anybody's leave to do anything. And mainly I don't have to depend on other folks for nothing, nor they on me."

"But that's not true, really. When folks had freights they depended on you and you on them, and now they don't have any freights for you to carry, you can't keep sailing anymore, can you? So you've been depending on folks all the time."

He studied on that a while, and then drew a long breath and let it out in a long sigh and said with an air of giving up the last of all that he held dear, "That's so."

"I always knew how you felt. Right from the beginning. Mother never really did understand, and she never quite forgave you for not going to my father's funeral or Frank's wedding or for not wanting to marry me. But I could always just see how you felt and how hard it all was for you, and I never blamed you, even if I wished so much you could be different."

He was silent a long while, thinking. Then he said, "I built the *Harraseeket*. I knew what was in every part of her and I knew that it was all right because I'd seen it was done right myself. If I had money to do with, I'd rebuild her now and she'd be her old self again and I'd know I'd be all right, never mind the weather."

"Well, you made me too, you know. And I don't mean all that silly advice you gave me! But do you remember those dresses you made me buy? I still have that one I put on first for you to see. When I want to feel the most myself I can I wear it, although it's pretty old and worn now. When I found out that a man as big and powerful as Myatt could be led around by me just being pretty, I thought being with him made things so simple and made me who I am. But when I finally learned my lesson about vanity, I kept thinking about how I used to want just to be your friend and companion. I can't stand to think of you dying unwanted when I want so much to be with you.

"I have a little cottage right up there on the hill, and we could live there. I don't have very much money, but it would be enough for us. And if I know you, you won't sit around moping long before you'll be doing something to turn a dollar. But it'll be up to you. You won't have to do anything until you want to. You can stay right away from everybody as much as you want."

He glanced around at her, his eyes glistening wet around the rims, and then he went back to looking out the port.

"That's pretty nice of you to be thinking of me," he said in a choked voice. "But I don't know. I'm pretty old to change my ways now. Settin' up there in a house . . . I don't know . . . "

"Leland, you have to change or die."

"I know it," he said after a few moments.

Leland clung to his beloved *Harraseeket* for another month, Ann visiting him there every day and gently talking to him about coming ashore to live with her. Then there was a blow and suddenly the *Harraseeket*'s seams opened, and she required continuous pumping just to stay even.

"You've got to do something with her," Ann said. "Or she'll go down right here in the harbor and you don't have the money to pay for floating her again. Why don't you put her up on the flats? Then you can decide what to do from there."

"If she goes on the flats she'll never come off."

Ann did not contradict him.

After three days of pumping, the *Harraseeket* began to settle slowly, and Leland finally hove short his anchor with Ann's help, and at high water slack they sailed the *Harraseeket* on her last voyage, to the flats. When she struck, she slid forward on the mud, slowing, and came finally to a stop.

Leland was shaky and fumbly and befuddled as they gathered up his things and loaded them into the yawl-boat. Then the time came to leave. The *Harraseeket*'s deck was already canting as the tide dropped from under her. Leland stood gazing around at everything that had been essential to his life for so many years.

"Come on," Ann said gently, and she put her arm around him.

"I don't know what the world's come to that there ain't no place in it for the *Harraseeket*," Leland said shakily, as he looked one last time around the deck of his old schooner.

Leland and Ann climbed down into the yawl-boat, and the now-antique one-lung engine settled into a steady popping as the last of the coastermen gave up command of his vessel.   – *End*